Beneath the Tamarisk Tree

The Story Of A Thief's Redemption

Rob Seabrook

malcolm down

PUBLISHING

24 23 22 21   7 6 5 4 3 2 1

First published 2021 by Malcolm Down Publishing Ltd
www.malcolmdown.co.uk
Registered Office: Welwyn Garden City, England

British Library Cataloguing in Publication Data
A catalogue record for this book is available from the British Library.

ISBN 978-1-915046-01-7

Cover design by Esther Kotecha
Cover illustration Ella Baldry
Art direction by Sarah Grace

Printed in the UK

A Note from the Author

The Tamarisk Tree

After the treaty had been made at Beersheba, Abimelech and Phicol the commander of his forces returned to the land of the Philistines. Abraham planted a tamarisk tree in Beersheba, and there he called upon the name of the LORD, the Eternal God. And Abraham stayed in the land of the Philistines for a long time. (Genesis 21:32-34)

The tamarisk tree is a hardy species. It has a deep tap root and small leaves that enable it to survive well in arid conditions. It can be pruned hard but will still flourish, sprouting from the trunk or even a stump.

Yet, when it flowers each spring, it sets a stunning display of abundant pink and white blooms. As well as this beauty, it will always be generous with the shade and cover it provides.

In chapter 21 of the book of Genesis, we hear about how Abraham planted a tamarisk tree. Twenty-five years previously he had been promised the land by God. Now he was standing on that land, having just negotiated a peace treaty with his neighbours. It is likely that he was standing there with his new baby son, Isaac, impossibly prophesied by

God to Abraham and Sarah, in their old age. This family gathering was taking place alongside the well that had just been given to him as a gift by his new neighbour, Abimelech.

Abraham then *'called upon the name of the* LORD*'*, remembering the great promises that had been made to him and the amazing faithfulness of his God. This was his 'promised land' for his promised descendants. Hence his response was to dedicate it all to the God of eternity.

He planted a tamarisk tree to commemorate this, marking a significant milestone for him. Abraham had been on a long journey, physically and spiritually. On this journey, that we read about in the book of Genesis, he had times when he lost his trust in God and tried to take control of his own destiny, rather than relying on the promises that God had made to him.

Abraham had sinned. But despite his transgressions, when he turned back to his God, he found him to be forgiving, faithful and true to his promises. This is also one of the key themes reflected in the story of 'The Penitent Thief' from Luke chapter 23, that this book is based on. The theme being that, up until the moment when we die, it is never too late to turn to our Saviour and receive salvation. Abraham understood this, knowing that his God was a loving Father, who had a plan, a purpose and intended good for him.

In planting the tamarisk tree Abraham was laying down a 'peace marker' in the desert. A peace agreement had been made with his new neighbours and also a covenant with his God. He was re-dedicating himself to his God for ever. His eternal God.

Abraham's well can still be visited in Israel today, complete with tamarisk trees nearby. It may or may not be the same well and is unlikely to be the very same tamarisk tree, but it represents the idea that we all share in the promises that God made to Abraham. The inheritance available to all descendants of Abraham is God's promise to abide in eternal peace.

The tamarisk tree is mentioned in this book as a beautiful piece of creation that grabs the attention of the main character. Whilst he is lost in the depths of rejection and squalor, it represents to him a promise that there is always hope. The hope of salvation and the promise of eternal life at Jesus' side. Like the tamarisk tree, we can survive in arid conditions, resilient through the pains that life can often throw at us, as long as we have this tap root of hope.

The start of this character's life in heaven has been wholly imagined in this book, whilst taking some inspiration from the glimpses that are available to read in the scriptures. There we can find a few clues as to how magnificent heaven may be, but the truth is that we don't know and won't know until we get there. If what is imagined here does not work with your own view of what heaven may be like, then I encourage you to imagine it for yourself. Read about the nature and intentions of God and his creations, then seek inspiration to fire up your own imagination, to form your own vision of what paradise may be like.

Every one of us has a background and story that has led us to be who we are today. A series of events, choices of our own or inflicted on us by others, that have taken us down paths to where we find ourselves now. We are not to judge each other. That is purely the role of Jesus, to be carried out when we stand before him at the judgment seat and recount all the details of our own story to him. Only then will we know that true and lasting peace that can be gleaned from coming under the cover of the tamarisk tree.

This book is ultimately an act of worship, to bring glory to God. It is attempting to help us understand more of who God is and what he had to endure for each of us. The story is fiction, a novel, taking inspiration from scripture. It is not a theological or academic work, so if there is anything that offends or upsets you, this is not the intention. If that happens, dismiss that aspect and move on, in the hope that the rest of the story can still offer you some insights and encouragements. There is so much we do not and cannot know about heaven, but no doubt it will be so much better than anyone on earth is able to describe or imagine.

Be encouraged to rest beneath the tamarisk tree – metaphorically but why not physically too! It is a place of peace, a place of agreement, a place where we can know the promises of an eternal God over all our lives.

.

Dedication

This book is dedicated to you, the reader.

As you read it, I pray that you will be blessed by the knowledge that whatever your history, background and situation, there is a love that penetrates, permeates and edifies.

I pray you know that you are worth everything to the One who created you.

Chapter 1
The Awakening

Jesus answered him, 'I tell you the truth, today you will be with me in paradise.' (Luke 23:43)

Consciousness was slowly returning to him, sense by sense. His eyes were still closed. He felt confused but safe. He could tell he was lying down, so warm, comfortable and relaxed. He recalled the Rabbi's words from just a few moments before and they echoed loudly in his mind.

He could feel the softest movement in the air, just a wafting across his face as if someone had quietly walked by. He began to feel the movement of his hair and the folds in his clothes catching the breeze. The air surrounding him was swirling back and forth across his body like the loveliest of summer breezes. Comforting and relaxing, initiating no hurry in him to move.

It felt safe and calm around him. He was still hearing the words of that promise that the holy man had made.

He opened one eye, just a little, like a young child pretending to be asleep. Peeking out through the smallest of gaps between his eyelids, he was in awe at the sight in front of him. The source of this refreshing breeze, rousing him from his unconsciousness, was like a vision from a dream. Stood before him was a creature, twice his height, clothed in a white flowing robe, edged with gold. Around its middle was a golden belt that gathered the garment in folds to its waist. He had never seen anything so white, so unblemished and pure. As bright as lightning in the night sky. But its colour was not just a plain white. The creature had an aura of pearlescent light refracting around it, creating so many shades of white that glinted and sparkled in all directions.

It had a human form, with magnificent wings protruding from its spine. It was towering above him as he lay on the ground, its back turned towards him and one shoulder dropped, so that it could lean the wings in towards him, directing the air towards where he was lying. He counted three pairs of wings on the creature's back. This was the source of the reviving breeze that was gently pulling him into a fuller awareness of his surroundings.

He was hearing a different sound from each pair of wings, as they beat in turn. 'Al-Tir-Ah', 'Al-Tir-Ah', 'Al-Tir-Ah'. He knew those words. 'Do not fear.' 'Do not fear.' 'Do not fear.' The words were carried on the air currents with every sequence, calming the fear that was threatening to consume him. He took a deep breath. Any instinct to flee was subdued.

He needed to gather his thoughts out of this confusion. *Where am I? What has happened to me?* He was not used to being out in the open like this. His impulse should be to escape and hide. That is what he had been doing his whole life.

He could no longer just glimpse at this wonder from behind the protection of his eyelids. He had to open both his eyes wide, to fully appreciate the majesty of this creature. It turned to face him and their eyes met. A friendly smile flashed across its face and for the briefest moment he thought that he recognised it. A familiar face. Someone he had seen before, maybe in a crowd or from a dream. *But how could that be?*

As he gazed up towards it, wide-eyed, the creature knelt down on the ground beside him. He cowered, not sure whether to expect the worst, but the creature held out its hand towards his face and tenderly touched his cheek with the back of its hand. He felt warmth and light and tranquillity.

Then in one swift movement it rose to its full height and launched straight up into the air. Its job was completed. All six wings beat in a sequence with immense power. It ascended high up into the sky directly above his head and then in a wide arc across to the horizon and beyond, departing in a glorious spectacle of light and sound.

He stared into the sky until it was out of sight. This extraordinary vision had done nothing to help him fathom whether this was reality or a dream.

He took another deep breath, relieved to be alone again. His ears were now waking up and he began to hear what sounded like flowing water. Quickly it became all consuming, the only sound he could hear, becoming louder and louder. The sound of gushing water filled the soundscape, as if calling out to him to attract his full attention.

He found the strength to sit up, so that he could see where he was. Just a short distance beyond his bare feet he saw a stream that was flowing with clear water. The sight and sound of this fresh water reawakened his desperate thirst, caused by the trauma he had just lived through.

The torture. The humiliation. The pain.

As he remembered that scene and what he had endured, the man's words returned to him again. He dared to wonder, just briefly, if maybe, by some miracle, they had come true. *Can I dare to believe that he was telling the truth? Surely not.* He knew who he was and the sort of life he had led. He had thought before that there was only ever going to be one outcome for a boy like him. But then the pain had gone. *Maybe I am in paradise?*

He was drawn back to the water and had to drink, but he was weak, without the strength to get to his feet. After what had happened, he was unsure if his legs would ever carry his weight or move without significant pain. He dropped onto his side and rolled over, so that he was face down on the grass. He could then push up onto his elbows and pull himself along the ground with his arms. His legs dragged along behind him the few feet towards the stream. When at the edge of the water, he could stay on his front with his head and arms over the bank, reach into the water and cup it up to his mouth.

It was the sweetest taste he had ever known. The moment the cool water touched his lips he felt refreshed. As he swallowed, life itself returned to his body. Just a mouthful seemed to permeate every fibre inside him. Every joint, bone and muscle seemed to gain form and strength. He felt stronger. He felt life returning. He felt alive again.

He looked down through the water. Unlike the streams he had known before with dirt or pebbles running along their bed, he could see thousands of lustrous stones that glistened and shone. Gemstones of all colours – jasper, diamonds, emeralds, topaz, crystals. He had never seen such riches. He knew his first instinct would usually have been to grab at them, to plunder. But at that moment his feelings were of intrigue and awe, mesmerised by the treasure. As he reached down to touch them, he found they were just out of his grasp, tantalisingly beautiful but beyond him.

He noticed his own reflection, mirrored in the surface of the water. He had so rarely seen his own face that to him this could have been a stranger staring back at him. The face he saw was not as thin as he remembered, the angular cheek bones no longer his main feature. He touched the flesh on his cheeks just to check it was really himself he was seeing. His face looked fuller than he remembered. His hair was short, black and clean, his beard was trimmed, coarser than before, no longer the fluffy, patchy beard of a youth. His bright, clear, brown eyes returned his own gaze.

With just those few mouthfuls of water he felt wholly revived. Not just his thirst quenched but his body felt healed and mended. He looked himself over and could see no obvious wounds, no dried blood or scabs. There was scarring on his wrist and feet where the nails had pierced him, but no other outward signs of the torture. *Maybe I have been here for a few weeks?*

With his strength returned, he sat up at the water's edge to compose himself. *How long have I been here?* Time was vague, not helped by this dream-like experience. That man had promised that it would be 'today'. *Is it still 'today'?* He had no concept of time. He could have been unconscious for minutes, hours or many days.

The water had worked its power in him and he felt he now had the strength to try to stand. His mind was cleared and he was sure that the mysterious creature must have been an illusion. Curiosity was getting the better of him and he needed to look around, to try to get some context to his surroundings. But as he tentatively stood to his feet and found his balance, the scene that unravelled in front of him was astounding. Any plan he had of trying to get a sense of perspective on the landscape rapidly evaporated.

He surveyed the stream immediately in front of him. It drew his gaze away, leading his eyes as it spread out across the flat plain that stretched before him for as far as he could see in any direction. As the water flowed, other streams joined it from all directions. They crossed the landscape like veins bringing the very lifeblood to the land. There were sections where the water was shallower and running faster, the light dancing on the ripples and rapids. In other parts the water was slowly meandering into pools, turning bluer as the water deepened.

Clean water had been such a rarity for him. With all these streams, here you could never go thirsty, never be unclean, never escape this life-giving flowing water. To him, this already formed a vision of paradise. The longer he stared at it, the more he could see the full extent of this network of streams and rivers.

And he was hearing them too. The multiple layers of sounds emanating from each course created a rising and falling, a crescendo of water music, with the sound of waterfalls rumbling, ocean waves crashing and rapids roaring, all creating harmonies that ebbed and flowed as if they were breath, bringing life to a body.

His thoughts began to deepen. *What if this is true? What if this really is what that man had promised to me? That man on the cross, the one they called Jesus. Is this what he meant when he told me, 'Today you will be with me in paradise'?*

He had been in excruciating pain at the time. He had been hallucinating from the dehydration and exhaustion. This could easily be one of those fantasies. But he had also heard the crowds cry out to him, calling him the Messiah, their Deliverer. *They had hope in him so maybe I can too?*

As he remembered the words of Jesus' promise, he found the vision before him open up even further. The magnitude of the landscape emerged into focus. The network of streams was flowing, forming its very foundation, but more of the picture was being revealed to him, layer by layer.

Between each stream there was grass. Mostly short and neat and perfect, but some areas were longer, forming meadows that swayed to the rhythms of the landscape. The movement gave the grass a depth of colour, hundreds of shades of green, the light dancing across it and through it to create a palette that any artist would long for.

As he looked closer he could see the flowers in the meadows were all unique. Not just different types of flowers, but each individually different, varying in hues that he had never seen before, unique in shape and pattern of their petals. The flowers lifted up their faces as if they were stretching their necks to seek out the light.

He could now see the trees and shrubs of all shapes and sizes that punctuated the vista. Many were planted alongside the streams, their roots feeding from the life-giving waters, their boughs dipping leaves, leaving a trail of colour on the surface of the water, as if melting.

Around him there were fruit trees in blossom, not just the usual pinks and whites, but also reds, blues, purples. These trees were in flower but also producing fruit at the same time. *Is this a place without seasons, without limits on growth?* The fruit looked perfect and bountiful, with so many varieties he had never seen before. It was a picture of perfection. He could easily believe that this was paradise.

The scent that the flora produced filled the air, the scent of a million flowers, all distinct, all filling his senses in unison. He had spent a life with the smell of decay and waste in his nostrils. The contrast was immense, with the fragrance from so many flowers and fruits producing a sweetness he could only compare to that of the fresh melons and peaches on a market stall, mixed with the soft, delicate, luscious scent of honeysuckle, only a thousand times more varied.

This wonderous landscape was in a constant state of abundant growth, flowering and fruiting, displaying its glory. Always productive and never dying. He could not spot any dead wood or even a fallen leaf from any of the trees and shrubs that filled his vision.

The melody from the water, that was continuously playing in the background, was joined by birdsong, singing a song to the water's tune. The more he listened, the more he began to hear new sounds joining in. Harmonies from the insects. He had only ever known the constant clicking of cicadas, but this was a swarm of insects, singing the same chorus.

He could even hear the leaves on the trees chiming away to the same anthem. Harmony after harmony as the whole landscape worshipped in agreement.

He turned his attention to the far distance. Beyond the plain of meadows and streams was a huge forest of much taller trees, taller than any he had seen or imagined, hundreds of feet high. Strong and majestic and powerful. At the foothills of a mountain range, the forest gave way to what looked like vineyards, growing up the gentle slopes in lines. Snow-capped mountains soared above, too high for a man to climb, too wide to go around. Towering waterfalls were cascading down the sides of the mountains, supplying the streams that spread across the landscape. Their spray rose into the air creating rainbows all around. He had heard stories of mountains but never seen anything so magnificent.

Bordering the whole landscape were four wide rivers, into which flowed the network of streams, taking the water off to whatever lay beyond.

He looked up to see the immense sky, towering above the mountains. Blue, but not simply a flat blue. A mixture of every shade of blue, with streaks of silver and gold, churning and dancing to the choruses being played out across the valley, moving in time to the heartbeat of the landscape. Watching the sky was mesmerising, the blues now melding with greens, purples, pinks, oranges and colours that he could not name, all shimmering and gently swirling. In the darker patches he could see sparkles, a little like stars but displaying their glory in a myriad of different colours.

This light was so different. He was used to shirking away from the daylight, keeping to the shadows. But the light was comforting and reassuring. It brought a tangible warmth. He could not see the sun or the source of the light, but it was all around, so powerful. Even the most densely leaved trees were producing no shadows on the ground. The light was so pure, enhancing every colour and detail with intensity.

As he looked more closely, he could see the light shining right through objects. He gasped as he studied a beautiful yellow flower, the size of his hand. The light saturated the petals, then seeped right through it to scatter a display of colour across the air like sunlight in a glass prism. He looked down at his hand. It was even casting the light through him. It was alive, showering wisps of colour all around. It was in everything and was giving life to everything.

This permeating light gave him a feeling he had rarely known before. Love. Love had been so elusive in his life, but he could just recognise it.

He was standing on the grass by the stream, turning and gazing at the wonders around him as each in turn stole his attention. He could hear the sounds from birds fluttering and dancing in the sky nearby. A happy sound.

Strength was returning to his body. He felt stronger and more whole than he had felt for many years. As he staggered around he was aware how difficult it was to walk, a result, no doubt, of the bones in his legs that had been broken. But he was more mobile than he expected.

His attention was caught again by the birds, hovering over a small hill, just a short distance away. A vantage point, to get a better view of the landscape. He walked uncertainly to the foot of the hill, habitually checking the landscape for any sign of danger, and began to slowly ascend towards the top.

As he neared the summit, where the birds, the white doves, were hovering overhead, he looked across and saw the figure of a man.

Chapter 2
A New Beginning

That if you confess with your mouth, 'Jesus is Lord,' and believe in
your heart that God raised him from the dead, you will be saved.
(Romans 10:9)

He paused in his tracks the moment he saw the man reclining on the grassy hillside. Doubt and mistrust raced back into his thoughts, chasing away any brief respite he had been allowing himself from his normal state of permanent alertness.

But it was too late. He had been spotted. The man smiled warmly and beckoned him over. He was reluctant, being out in the open like this was unnerving and he instinctively wanted to flee. His mind raced to assess the situation. He checked behind. He hesitated, his eyes darting back and forth, scanning to see if there was anyone else nearby. The man waved him over again. He swallowed and took a few tentative steps forwards.

As he approached, he looked into the man's eyes and to his astonishment he recognised him. He knew immediately that it was him, the Rabbi, Jesus. Those clear brown eyes unchanged from what seemed like just a few moments ago, when he had witnessed life leaving his body. Those eyes drew him in, an attraction he could not yet understand.

But he had seen him die. *What sort of illusion is this?* This man was certainly alive, breathing, smiling, reclining in the meadow whilst the grass and flowers danced and giggled excitedly all around him.

There was clearly no hiding the look of astonishment and bewilderment on his face.

'Welcome,' said the Rabbi. 'I see the angel has revived you. Are you rested?'

'Yes, I think so.' *So that was an angel!* When he spoke, he was surprised that his voice was sounding so steady and calm. The simple act of speaking out loud made this scene seem so much more real. *Perhaps this is not a dream?*

'Come sit with me. Don't be afraid.'

The last time he had seen the Rabbi, his body was broken, he was bloodied, bruised and naked. Now he was healed and whole, hardly recognisable from when they were both hanging on crosses outside the city walls. He was clothed in white robes, glowing, with the purple scars on his wrists and ankles clearly visible from where the nails had been driven through him.

He stole a quick glance at his own wrists and could see similar scars. He had been there.

Despite just having shared the intimacy of death together, he still did not know who the Rabbi was or how to address him.

'Who are you?' he blurted out. 'I mean I . . . I don't know what to call you. I mean, I don't know your name,' he added, realising this was already too close to him asking that one question he had spent his whole life avoiding.

'I have many names. For you at this moment, I am Yeshua. I am your rescuer. The name you heard me called before is Jesus, your salvation.'

Jesus looked at him, eyebrows raised as if to ask *and you are?*

He hesitated. His ingrained habit of never sharing his name was going to be a difficult one to shake off.

'And what do you want me to call you?' Jesus persisted.

Looking down at the ground, cautiously he said, 'My name is Dismas.'

He could not look up. He waited for the inevitable response when someone heard his name. He anticipated the shame and embarrassment that would overwhelm him, even when he heard it himself. This time though, there was nothing. No reaction, no comments. He relaxed a little.

He stood there next to Jesus, his mind beginning to process the situation. With a cautious smile of realisation daring to dawn across his face as he allowed himself to think it may actually be true. *Maybe, then, this is paradise?* He needed to be certain.

'You are the same man that was next to me on the cross?'

Jesus nodded.

Warily he continued, 'So, has your promise come true? Am I really here with you in paradise?'

'It is as I promised. Yes, you are here in paradise with me,' said Jesus reassuringly.

Dismas felt a relief wash over him. He was not an emotional man. Emotions were a luxury he could rarely afford and habit was forcing him to suppress the feelings. Tears had begun to form in his eyes. Tears of relief from the pain of his existence. He checked himself, fighting them off. He was not ready for crying yet.

'I have so many questions,' but his voice just tailed off, lost in his thoughts. The scale of what was happening to him was too immense to understand. There was a pause as they looked at each other.

'Why don't you sit down for a while?' said Jesus calmly.

Dismas nodded and sat on the grass next to Jesus. He had never walked on grass before and the ground was warm and soft, so much more comforting than any of his usual resting places. The two of them sat in silence on the hillside. Jesus knew that Dismas needed some time to settle. There was no hurry. Dismas was lost in his thoughts for a few moments.

Amongst the sounds reverberating around him, Dismas was able to pick out a voice in the distance. Someone else was here, singing, harmonising with the sounds of the landscape. The song grew louder as it approached and, looking over Jesus' shoulder, he saw a figure coming around the hillside. It was a little girl, skipping through the meadow, singing a sweet melody.

When she saw Jesus, she beamed a grin and squealed with delight. She broke into a run and raced towards him. At the sound of her sweet voice, Jesus turned and jumped to his feet to greet her. He was just in time to catch her in his arms, as she threw herself into his embrace. Her arms encircled his neck, his arms wrapped around her back, in an act of pure joy and love. As they embraced, there was an explosion of light from them both that rose up and intertwined as it spiralled skywards.

Jesus looked so pleased, actually glowing with joy. He whispered a few words into her ear that Dismas could not hear. Jesus lowered her to her feet and they both turned to look at Dismas, holding hands. Their intimacy looked so natural; the warmth was tangible. As she glanced at Dismas, their eyes met and something inside him leaped in recognition, as though his soul was connecting with her. He was captivated by her presence, an aura surrounding her as though she was giving off a powerful fragrance.

'This is my companion,' said Jesus as the two of them settled back down to the ground next to Dismas. 'The Spirit of God. The Holy Spirit,' he added. 'The Spirit can take many forms, to suit the task that needs to be completed. Sometimes those forms are visible, some may not be, but the Spirit always knows what is needed.'

The Spirit of God, thought Dismas. *How could I be in the presence of the Spirit of God?* He felt uncomfortable being close to anything that was holy. *Surely I should not be allowed to be here?* He clearly needed more reassurance from Jesus.

'You are in paradise now. Remember I gave you my promise. It is the truth and this truth will set you free.'

Truth and honesty had been rare companions throughout his life. Trust was even more of a stranger. There had been many times when Dismas did not know what the truth was. Most of his life had been founded on lies and deceit. But as he looked Jesus in the eye again, he felt as though everything he had ever done, felt and had experienced was fully known and understood. That very idea caused in him a wave of shame to bubble to the surface.

'I am not sure I should really be here,' he said nervously.

'That's not unusual. Why do you feel like that?'

'There was a good reason why I was hanging on that tree next to you. It was my due punishment. I have not done anything to deserve to be here.'

'Nor has anyone else.'

Dismas did not really understand.

'Why do you think you don't deserve to be here?' These words of Jesus were so gently spoken.

Dismas pondered how to respond, not really wanting to confess the memories that had begun to flash through his mind.

'I am not the sort of person who should be in paradise. People like me just don't deserve it. The life I lived did not deserve any reward.'

'Why don't you start at the beginning of your story?'

A look of fear dawned on his face. Dismas had never told anyone his story, even if he was able to remember it at all. The thought of recounting it filled him with embarrassment and shame. Jesus, still reclining, held out his hand. Dismas was drawn to it, holding out his own hand. As their hands touched, he was filled with a peace that put flight to the shame and fear that had begun to engulf him.

Jesus pulled Dismas in closer, so he too had no option but to recline on the ground, facing Jesus. All the time Jesus held eye contact with Dismas, which he found unnerving. He was not used to looking anyone in the eye, but as he looked into the gaze of Jesus, the gentleness that emanated from him was calming and reassuring.

'Relax,' said Jesus. 'Tell me about your beginning.'

Dismas took a deep breath.

'I only know about my birth from what my uncle told me. My father was his youngest brother. I never knew my mother and only met my father once.

'My uncle told me that I killed my mother.' As he spoke out these words a tear formed in his eye. The Holy Spirit looked concerned, stood up and moved to settle closer to Dismas. She reached over to wipe the tear from his cheek. He did not recoil from it. Her touch was soft and calming.

'Tell me what it was that your uncle said to you,' prompted Jesus gently.

'My uncle was the eldest son in his family,' Dismas slowly continued, finding it so hard to tell this story. 'There were seven of them, all boys. My father was the youngest. My mother died. I don't remember her. At first my uncle would tell me that my father was broken-hearted and could not look after me. So I had to live with him and my aunt.'

Dismas paused, hoping that this would be enough. But looking at Jesus' expression, clearly he was expecting more. *I can't believe I'm telling anyone this*, Dismas thought to himself, and continued.

'But as I got older, he would tell me that my mother died when I was born. She died giving birth to me. When my uncle got angry, he would say that my mother never even saw me and that my father could not bear me to even be in his house. So when I was born I was taken straight to my uncle's house.' There was so much more to this story, but he could not speak it out yet.

'Tell me what your uncle and aunt were like,' Jesus said. Dismas was reluctant but continued.

'They did not like me. They never made me welcome. They were old and their children were much older than me. They had seven or eight and none of them lived in the house anymore. They would come and visit, but not take much notice of me. My uncle and aunt clearly did not want me to be there. I was an expense and a burden that had been forced upon them. They probably felt they were done with children but here they were, having me to look after.'

Dismas was surprised how easy it was for him to talk like this. He had never spoken this much before. He carried on.

'My uncle always seemed to be angry. I think he enjoyed telling me how much my father didn't want me. He would say it with a smile on his face. I am sure he liked being cruel. When he was feeling angry, he would complain about everything, shout and swear at my aunt, hit her and throw things at me. He would scream at me to get out of his house. Tell me he was not surprised my father did not want me. I was vermin, a rat who brought death.'

'You said you met your father once?'

Dismas looked pained at the memory. It was not a happy one. He took another deep breath, stared at the ground and continued.

'I must have been about three or four years old.' He started nervously, really not wanting to share the story. 'I had been out of the house running some errand with my aunt. When we got back home, we heard raised voices from inside. We went in and my uncle was there with another man. We had clearly interrupted their argument. My uncle looked alarmed. I have never seen anyone so full of fury as the other man. As we stood in the doorway, I could sense something was wrong and I looked up at my aunt. I remember her looking back down at me with a face full of panic.

'The two men hurriedly stood up. The man that I did not know glared at me directly in the eye as he stormed towards the door. I remember that look in his eyes. The hatred, the fury, the disgust all focused on me.'

Dismas paused as the pain simmered inside him. He knew he had to finish the story now.

'My uncle shouted out, "Go easy on him. It's not his fault." The man said nothing. As he brushed past me he looked down, spat at my face and left the house. My uncle followed close behind, pausing as he got to me. He looked at me, his eyes welling up with tears, as he told me that the other man was my father.

'I remember being unable to move, as my father's phlegm ran down my face.'

*

They sat there in silence for a few moments, whilst this story reverberated around his mind.

'I think that was the only time I ever saw my father.'

'Being a parent is such an important job,' responded Jesus. 'That man was not behaving as a father. We will be your Father from now on,' and the Spirit looked up at them both excitedly.

'I am going to ask you an important question. I know that you had faith in me when you were on the cross. Your heart turned to me then, which is why you are here now. You called out to me in hope and you are now here with me in paradise. You can see plainly for yourself that my promise has come true. Do you still believe that I am who my followers said I was?'

Dismas had to think back to the cross. To remember the names used by Jesus' followers that were mixed in with the accusations and insults that were hurled at him as he hung there. His accusers mocked and called him 'The King of the Jews', whilst his followers called him 'The Messiah'. They believed Jesus was their Saviour and yes, he did too.

Dismas had to force himself beyond his suspicious and untrusting nature. If he was in paradise, which he did believe, and with all that he had seen since he had regained consciousness, he felt it could only be the truth.

'Yes,' said Dismas, a little tentatively.

'That's all we need,' Jesus said softly. 'You have confessed the truth. So it shall be as I said. From now on we are your Father.'

Dismas believed what Jesus was saying to him, even though he could not see how it was possible. He had to learn how to trust. To discover what it felt like to rely on someone, to not be afraid of their motives. To not be fearful of disappointment or being let down by everyone.

'We are going to do something important now,' said Jesus as he rose to his feet. 'Step over here with me.'

Dismas stood slowly, his legs stiff. Jesus placed his hands on Dismas' shoulders and guided him down the slope, towards the nearest stream. On reaching the bank, Jesus released Dismas, but he continued, stepping down into the water. Dismas was left standing on the bank.

'Now don't be afraid,' said Jesus, turning back to look at Dismas. 'Put your trust in me. I want you to come into the water with me.'

Dismas hesitated. Trusting was difficult. He was not in control. He had never been in water before. He had never bathed or washed. The water looked deep and frightened him. He stood there like a petrified animal, his heart pounding in his chest. He was fighting every instinct to run. He looked down at Jesus who was surrounded by the clear sparkling water.

'It will be fine,' and Jesus offered him a reassuring look. 'We would like to baptise you.'

It was a word that Dismas had heard before, but he had no idea what it meant or what was involved.

'We want to baptise you into our family. Baptism is a rite of adoption. It is a way of showing us that you want to be a part of our family. A way of leaving your old life behind and enabling you to press on into a new life here in paradise.'

To Dismas, this sounded good. He had thought there was only one way to escape from his old life. It had been a prison with no reprieve. If this man was his Saviour, then he had to trust. At the very least he had nothing to lose. He took a deep breath.

The step down into the water was going to be a big step. Leaving his old life behind was all very well, but he had a lot of baggage, much of it a comfortable and familiar companion. It may not have been good, but it was part of him.

As every doubt flashed through his mind he hesitated. In the midst of his reluctance, he felt the presence of the Holy Spirit standing alongside him. He looked down into her eyes and she smiled with so much compassion and understanding that his fears melted. He could not feel threatened with her at his side. She gently took his hand in hers and guided him to the water's edge.

Dismas felt comfort and peace. They stood together in the shallows. The stream felt cool and calming, the water tickling around his toes.

Jesus took his other hand and led him towards the deeper water in the centre of the stream. He was fascinated by this new sensation, seeing his feet glide for the first time through the crystal clear, pure water. The gemstones beneath his feet felt soft with no sharp edges. When they reached the middle of the stream they paused, the water waist deep around them.

As Dismas looked down at his legs in the water, he started to see red swirls emanating from Jesus' body, what looked like his blood mixing with the water.

With Jesus on one side of him, they each placed one hand on Dismas' back, between his shoulder blades, and their other hand on his elbow.

'Dismas. You have said that you believe in me. Are you happy for me to now baptise you?'

I'm not sure I know what baptism means.

'Yes, I suppose so,' he replied.

'Then I baptise you into our family. From now on, you are washed clean. Your family is complete. We are your Father.'

Jesus gently tipped Dismas backwards until he was completely submerged beneath the waters. It was just a brief moment under the water for him, but it felt like an eternity. As the water flowed over and around him, from his head to his feet, he felt a change taking place. Starting at his head, blackness, like liquid filth, began to seep from within him. It was not from the outside, but from his inside. As it seeped from his head, this ink-like substance merged with the blood-like swirls coming from the body of Jesus. As the two colours melded with the stream water, they were diluted and disappeared. Gone.

This discharge worked its way down his body, mostly from his head, but as that subsided there was more from his shoulders, arms, body and legs. Eventually his feet let out their filth and the process was complete.

Dismas was cleansed and invigorated. Feelings he had never known and could not explain. He felt a wholeness had been restored to him. The rejection he had carried as a curse since his birth, was gone.

As he lifted Dismas back to his feet, Jesus declared, 'You are our son, whom we love and we are well pleased with you.'

At these words, the Spirit started to sing over Dismas, a chorus so beautiful that it seemed to harmonise with his soul. As the anthem grew, she lifted her arms, up towards the doves that were hovering in the sky above. She was directing the birds to encircle them as they stood there in the water. All corners of the landscape joined her in numerous harmonies, building to an immense crescendo that filled the skies in celebration, with all the power focused on Dismas.

As the melodies eventually subsided, they walked through the water towards the bank on the other side of the stream. They stepped out and settled on the grass, in the warmth. The doves landed and settled down on the ground around them. They were instantly dry.

Chapter 3
Crowned with Splendour

You will be a crown of splendour in the Lord's *hand, a royal diadem in the hand of your God. No longer will they call you Deserted, or name your land Desolate.* (Isaiah 62:3-4)

They sat still and quiet for a while. Jesus was giving Dismas the time he needed to think through what had just happened, but he remained close by. Rest was important in heaven to allow souls to adjust. Dismas was trying to understand emotions and feelings that had been deeply hidden or were even entirely new to him. His mind needed re-training. It had been his habit to build an impenetrable, protective barrier around himself, which needed to be torn down.

Sitting there in the warmth and safety, Dismas rested peacefully, processing his thoughts and allowing them to wander. He felt that for the first time in his life something good had happened to him. *How is it that I have ended up in paradise?*

He contemplated the part of his life story that he had begun to recount to Jesus. He seemed so far away from that world now.

Dismas lay back into the warmth of the riverbank and closed his eyes.

Everything around him was a comfort to his senses. His thoughts took him back to those early days.

When he lived with his aunt and uncle, he had never really understood why he was there. It was never explained to him. Life became a constant confusion with every aspect fuelled by worry, driven by fear.

One of his earliest memories was from one sunny morning, walking through his neighbourhood, trotting along beside his aunt. As a youngster he was always reaching out to hold her hand, but she would never take it for very long, always finding a reason to let him go. He took to gripping it as tight as he could, but she would just complain he was hurting her and shake him free.

Along their street, they heard someone call out.

'He's growing taller now,' a neighbour shouted out as they walked past the open doorway to her home.

'He is,' replied his aunt. 'But of course, the bigger he gets the more he eats,' she complained. They paused briefly to chat.

'Is he a greedy boy then?' the neighbour continued accusingly. Both ladies tutted.

'Any extra mouth to feed is a problem,' his aunt said in a resigned manner. 'Especially at the moment.'

Dismas remembered his cheeks reddening and staring at the ground, unable to look at either woman.

'It's a shame, isn't it?' The two ladies chatted for a few minutes, whilst Dismas ignored the rest of the conversation.

They finished the pleasantries and as Dismas and his aunt walked away there was just a look of pity on the neighbour's face.

'Why?' Dismas tentatively said to his aunt, as they wandered a little further down the street.

'Why what?' she snapped back.

'Why is it so bad for us now?'

'Because of your uncle's arm, of course,' came the angry reply, as though he was stupid.

Dismas knew that something was wrong with his uncle, even though he had never been told what it was. His uncle used to go out to work and when he came home he would proudly brag about the beautiful houses he had helped to build. But he had not been out to work for a few weeks. Dismas had overheard them talking about how his uncle's arm had been crushed when a pile of stones had collapsed on him. Dismas sometimes caught himself staring at it, as it hung limply down from his uncle's shoulder, dead and useless inside his sleeve.

After his uncle's arm died things became worse in their home. Anger, shouting and arguing became the norm. Fear moved in. He discovered at an early age that he had become a burden to his aunt and uncle and they did little to prove him wrong.

Even on the rare occasions when there were happy times in that house, he never felt fully included as a member of that family. When festivals filled the city with excitement, sometimes there would be celebrations in their home. Others in the family would visit the house, like his aunt's and uncle's children. But Dismas would never be permitted to recline at the table with the adults. As the only young child there, he would have to sit on the floor in the dark corners of the room, generally missing out on the feasting.

Birthday celebrations were rare, but certain years demanded recognition. One year, he remembered his aunt preparing a special feast to celebrate his uncle's birthday. Their small home was filled with friends and family, with feasting and singing. Everyone was happy. Dismas watched from the fringes.

As the party subsided, in his innocence he walked across the room, stood next to his uncle and asked, 'When will it be my birthday?'

The party went silent and his uncle's face changed as the anger boiled up inside him. It was released in a tirade of abuse.

'How dare you talk about your birthday,' he spat venomously. The veins on his neck were bulging, fiercely pumping blood to his reddened face. 'You will never have a birthday. That wretched day you were born will never be celebrated. You brought disaster on that day and now you ruin this day too.'

His aunt stepped in, gathered up Dismas and quickly shuffled him out of the room, as the others came around his uncle to calm him down. She had decided to protect him that time.

'Never mind,' she said, trying to calm the young lad from his sobbing. 'It's been difficult recently.'

'Why is it always my fault?'

'It isn't. Sometimes people say things they don't really mean.'

'Everyone hates me.'

'Well, I am sure your mother would have loved you.'

At this, Dismas looked up, startled that his mother was even mentioned. His aunt was looking into the distance, as though remembering a happy thought.

'I don't even know her name,' he said, half asking.

His aunt paused, not sure whether to continue or not. But perhaps it was time.

'Her name was Ilana. Your father had known her since she was a young girl and he loved her so very much. We could all see how precious she was to him.' And there her brief daydream ended, as she looked back down at the young boy.

'Never mind,' she said. And that was that.

*

These early memories were difficult for Dismas to recollect. He opened his eyes and sat up. He found he was still on the riverbank, Jesus and the Holy Spirit close by, as though keeping watch over him while he was lost in these memories. A pang of conviction crept into his mind. *Should I really be remembering all of this distress when I'm in heaven?* A worried look appeared on his face and he started to search his mind for any positives from his past.

He looked back up to Jesus and, thinking out loud, he said, 'I suppose my aunt occasionally tried to be kind,' he was trying to be generous. But he could only think of one other example, and this one pained him to recount. He fell silent and looked away.

'Don't worry,' said Jesus. 'It is fine to tell us this part.'

Dismas knew it was a part of the story that needed to be told.

'I remember once she told me how she liked my name,' he blurted out hurriedly. 'She said Dismas meant "sunset" and that sunsets were beautiful. She said it was an honour to be named after something so colourful. But . . .'

Then his voice tailed off. He did not want to recall this next part of his story. He wanted to forget, to move on, to never have to think about it again.

Jesus looked at him with those penetrating eyes. Although Dismas knew it would hurt to relive it, he did owe it to Jesus to carry on.

'I need to tell you some more,' he said, as he summoned all his courage. Jesus smiled encouragingly and gave Dismas every bit of his attention.

'I don't think my uncle liked it when my aunt showed me any kindness. He would shout at her if she ever gave me any nice morsels of food, or even if he found me sleeping wrapped in a cloak. I was meant to sleep on the dirt.

'When he heard my aunt say to me how nice my name was, he was filled with fury. He shouted across the room to her, "You know that's not his real name! Tell him his real name!"

'"No! Don't be so cruel! He doesn't need to know the truth," she shouted back.

'"Then I will," he screamed. "Dismas is not your real name. It's the name your father gave you when you killed your mother. Your real name will never be heard."'

Dismas had never told anyone this part of the story. Staring at the ground, he continued 'My aunt did try to stop him, but my uncle screamed out some more. "And you know that 'Dismas' does not just mean 'sunset'. It's not a beautiful thing. It's the word for when life and light disappear, when the sun is extinguished. For you it means 'death'. You are called 'death' because it's your fault that the sun went down on your mother's life. Your fault that she died. You killed her. You caused her to return to dust. That's why you are called 'death.''"

It was so painful for Dismas to get these words out. It was the first time he had ever repeated them out loud. They had been resounding in his head, haunting his thoughts through every day of his life, but they had never been allowed out.

'That was when I was maybe seven or eight.'

'I remember that day,' said Jesus, with a tear on his own cheek now. 'That one especially hurt.'

Dismas carried on, relieved that finally speaking out these things was in some way dealing with them. It helped him to warm to this new role of being the storyteller.

'When my uncle told me this it was like a spear piercing my heart. I ran. I ran and never looked back. I ran out of the house, down the street and just kept running. I didn't care. I had no intention of going back. I wanted to run away from my life. I wanted to get lost. I wanted to never be able to find my way back there. I ran through busy streets, people going about their own business and no one noticing me. When I was far enough away from them, I turned into a narrow dark alley, away from the light and noise of the street. Into the dark and the silence.

'I was breathing heavily, tears streaming down my face. I remember thinking that there was no point in running any more, that they wouldn't bother to follow me anyway. They would be glad I had gone. I stopped in that alley, crouched down in the shadows, looked into the dirt and sobbed. That was the last time I cried.

'From that moment, I hated my name. I vowed to myself that I would try not to tell it to anyone. If I told someone what I was called, they were bound to say, "What a lovely name, Dismas, named after the sunset." But all it would do is remind me of the death I had brought to my mother. So I simply stopped using any name. I stopped telling anyone what I was called. I had no name.' His voice tapered off as he was lost in the thought of what it had meant to him to be nameless.

Dismas looked up from the ground and noticed they both had tears on their cheeks now. Jesus turned to the Spirit, who had been quietly listening to every word.

'I need your help with this one,' he said as he settled back down to his reclined position opposite Dismas. She squealed with excitement and leaped to her feet. She knew what to do. She stood up and skipped off through the meadow that surrounded them, picking flowers and long blades of grass.

As she walked through the meadow, she sang a melody that mesmerised Dismas, soothing him from the inside. He felt at peace in her presence. To him she appeared so innocent and unthreatening. He watched as the flowers leaned in towards her, as though they wanted to be chosen. Every time she picked a stem, the plant would send out another bud, that would burst open a replacement straight away. Life was conquering death in every facet of this enchanted land.

She collected a large armful of the beautiful blooms and danced back to the riverbank, swirling and twirling through the grass and flowers. She sat down cross legged between Jesus and Dismas and placed the picked flowers on the ground. She then took each uniquely beautiful flower and began to weave them into a circle, with the grasses, to create a garland. They were both mesmerised by her joy, always humming, lost in her creativity. As the garland took shape, even though they were picked, the flowers were still living, swaying excitedly as though anticipating an even more important purpose.

Jesus and Dismas both remained silent, engrossed in this creation being so expertly crafted. Once finished, she held it up in front of her face with both hands and inspected it. She looked at Jesus with a broad smile.

'It is ready,' she announced, and passed it to Jesus. He gave her a loving look of approval.

'Perfect!' He stood up and took it from her. He then turned towards Dismas.

'This is for you. When someone receives a new name, they should also be crowned.'

Dismas was confused again.

'How can you give me a new name?'

'Well, we have many names. We also have the authority to name everyone. We want you to be known by your rightful name. In our Book of Life, Dismas is not the name we have written down for you.'

Is my real name really written in God's Book of Life?

'Stand,' said Jesus softly and Dismas rose stiffly to his feet; the two men stood facing each other.

'Your name is not Dismas. That name has been a curse for you. That curse is now broken and is no longer yours to bear.'

Jesus took the garland of flowers in both hands and placed it on Dismas' head, as if crowning a king. As the flowers touched his hair, Dismas felt a release, a weight lifting from his mind.

'Your name is Habib. Habib means "beloved" and you have always been our beloved.'

A sense of elation raced through his whole body.

'Habib,' he said to himself out loud. He liked this new name. It felt right. He was not unhappy to shed the old name. This was a fresh start.

'Habib. My name is Habib,' he repeated, to make sure it stuck.

'Habib, I want you to have this,' said Jesus, presenting to him a polished white pebble. It was perfectly round and on it there was embossed black lettering that spelled out his new name.

'This is to help you always remember who you really are.'

Habib took it from Jesus and looked at his name inscribed on the smooth white stone. He ran his finger across the letters. It was the most beautiful thing he had ever owned.

'Thank you. This is like treasure for me.'

He placed it in the breast pocket of his tunic, close to his heart.

Habib, who was hardly accustomed to wearing flowers, was standing on the bank of the river feeling like a king. His crown gave him a feeling of protection around his head, a warmth that was cradling and mending him. It was as though a yoke had been lifted from his shoulders and he could at last stand tall and proud of who he was.

Jesus stepped forward and embraced him. In that embrace he felt a depth of relationship that he had never thought possible. He closed his eyes and allowed the embrace to completely envelope him. He breathed out and relaxed, feeling a safety and comfort that he had never known, not even as a babe in arms. He was physically safe. He felt that Jesus knew his every thought and feeling, every word and deed from his past. He understood it all. There were no secrets, no shame, no fear. All was being put right. His identity was being renewed.

Jesus' arms were wrapped around Habib's shoulders, pulling him in close. He lifted one hand and tenderly brushed his fingers through Habib's hair, as a parent would comfort their child. Habib relaxed into the intimacy of the moment, quite comfortable in allowing Jesus to stroke his head.

'Every hair on your head is so precious to me. Each one was created and is perfect. Every part of you is as Father intended it to be. All that you are is so precious to us.'

Jesus let him go and stepped back. Habib remained standing there for a while, lost in his own thoughts, marvelling at what he had experienced, amazed that he could feel this sort of happiness.

He did not know how long he was standing there for. Time had lost its meaning. But one thing he was now certain of – he knew exactly who Jesus was.

Chapter 4
Alone in the Shadows

For we will all stand before God's judgment seat. It is written: 'As surely as I live,' says the Lord, 'Every knee will bow before me; every tongue will confess to God.' So then, each of us will give an account of himself to God. (Romans 14:10b-12)

Habib gradually became aware again of his surroundings. He was now alone, still standing beside the stream with the stunning landscape opening up before him. Having always had the instinct to seek solitude, he found it curious that he now craved the company of Jesus.

In his heart he wanted to rest, enjoy this beautiful environment and spend some time simply getting used to being Habib. He kept repeating the name to himself, worried that he may forget it. As he did so he put his hand to his breast pocket, to check his precious white stone was still there. He was standing tall, out in the open, not skulking in shadows like he used to. He felt bold and confident, so content with being this new creation. And as for being in heaven, all his senses were now alive to its miracles. The very thought of it made him smile.

He had not moved far from where he had first woken up and although his body was getting stronger, he still felt uncertain on his legs, staggering like a new-born foal. His legs were no longer broken, but were stiff and weak, so he could not wander too far, despite his newly discovered appetite to explore.

A short distance away he spotted a wooded area that intrigued him, with more trees than Habib had ever seen before. He had to take a closer look. The trees rose up from the meadow, with young saplings at its border, gently swaying. Behind them increasingly older, larger trees formed the dense wood.

Habib approached and as he stepped amongst the younger trees on the edges, they leaned apart to allow him through. When he reached the point where the trees were just a little taller than him, he paused and peered through them. They were growing too thickly for him to see very far ahead, so he cautiously had to edge in deeper. They made him feel safe, enveloping him behind and in front. It was not getting darker. The light did not reduce, even though the trees were close together. They did not cast any shadows.

A little way into the woods, he came to a clearing where the most ancient trees suddenly gave way to a meadow of long grass, speckled with dancing flowers. The area was about the size of the largest market square he used to prowl around, with a stream meandering through the middle. The clearing was punctuated with twelve large rocks, each the height of his waist, but broad and deep enough for three or four people to lounge on. Each was crafted from a different shade and pattern of what looked to him to be brightly coloured marble. Shades of marble he had never seen even on the most ornate porticos of the palaces in Jerusalem. Along the facing edge of each rock there was carved an inscription, words that Habib could not read.

To Habib, the most beautiful rock was a rich deep blue colour, polished and shining with shades of azure and purples, flecks of silver and gold glinting in the vibrant light. On it sat Jesus and above his head there appeared to be flames in the air, tongues of fire dancing above him. Inside, Habib's heart skipped as he could sense the presence of the Holy Spirit nearby.

As he approached, Jesus looked up and beamed a welcoming smile.

'Habib! It is so good to see you again.'

'Thank you,' although Habib felt as though he had interrupted. 'I am sorry to disturb you.'

'It is our pleasure to see you. You haven't disturbed us. We were just praying.'

'Praying? Why would you need to pray in heaven?'

'Praying is what I do here. We continually pray for everyone.'

It was a baffling conversation for Habib. The only praying he had seen before was when priests would stand outside the temple, dressed in their clean, long-flowing robes, praying in loud voices to ensure that everyone could hear. They would appear as pious as they were able, making sure that they were the centre of attention, with their wealth on full display. They would be surrounded by their pupils, nodding in agreement to every phrase, asking their God to 'cleanse the poor', 'feed the hungry' or 'save your chosen people'. Prayer only ever appeared to be abstract, irrelevant and disconnected hot air.

Feeling like he should make some conversation, he found himself saying, 'That rock you are sitting on is so wonderful.'

'It is made of a stone called lapis lazuli.'

Habib was struck by the beauty of the stone and the setting. He gazed around in wonder.

'What is this place for?'

'This is a special place. We love to spend time here. This is where people find it easiest to remember all that has happened before they came to heaven. Everyone has a plinth on which they can rest and reminisce. A chance to gather all their memories and thoughts into an order, to share their life experiences with us so as to make sense of it.'

Beneath the Tamarisk Tree

'It is so different here to what I am used to.'

Jesus looked him in the eye and smiled at him again. 'Yes. What do you find most different?'

He thought about this. *How could I pick just one thing?* Then it came to him.

'The light, I think. I used to spend most of my life hiding away during the daylight, trying not to be noticed. I would find a quiet place to rest, maybe sleep for a few minutes if there was no danger nearby. I would have to stay awake at night, in the dark, to keep safe. I didn't see much daylight. I am going to have to get used to being seen in the light.'

'I love it when you talk to us. It is so good for you to share with us all the details of your past. Come. Sit. Tell us some more about your life.'

Jesus beckoned Habib to sit down next to him. No one had taken any interest in Habib before. He sat down on the plinth alongside them, feeling like royalty sat on a throne.

'What do you want to hear about?'

'Tell us what happened after you ran away to the streets.'

Habib took a deep breath and started to recount more of the story.

*

On the day when he first ran away from his uncle and aunt, that narrow, dark alley where he had found refuge became his home for a few days. It was really just a gap between two houses, where the household waste would be dumped. It was hardly wide enough for a man to walk down without his shoulders touching both walls. The intense smell of decay gradually dissipated as his mind blocked it out. The rats scurried about nervously, not used to sharing their territory with anyone. He soon learned to kick out at them when they got too brave. But the alleyway was undisturbed by other people and he was hidden away, so it served his purposes well.

Dismas had no idea how many days or nights had passed since he first took refuge there, sobbing into the dirt. There had been times

44

when it was dark and times when there was complete blackness. Times when it was cool and times when he was overcome with shivering coldness. These days marked the beginning of the slow disintegration of his humanity.

It was extreme thirst that eventually pulled him out from the shadows. He was curled up tight in the dark, his shivering preventing him from sleeping. As the very first watery light of the day began to appear, in the distance he could hear the sounds of the city starting to rise. He realised he either had to leave now to find water or he would die there. He inched his way to the end of the alley, blinking into the street, the sunlight starting to glow against walls opposite. He stepped out and edged cautiously along the shadowy side. There were very few people out this early in the morning and to his relief, those that were there simply ignored him as they went about their business.

That first time he emerged, he skulked along the street for a few minutes before he happened upon the entrance to a house. He peered in and listened. All seemed quiet. He sneaked silently into the courtyard where the large clay jars of water were stored outside the door to the home. He put his hand in one of the jars, scooped the cool water to his mouth and drank hurriedly.

From inside he heard a girl call out, 'I'll fill the bucket.' As he heard the latch of a door lift, he darted away unnoticed.

His days soon turned into weeks as he found a routine. He became skilled at avoiding any other human contact, developing the instincts of a rat; in all situations he would have an escape route in mind, so as to scuttle away at the first sign of being discovered. This fear of being caught became a permanent companion. Dismas learned to be vigilant, every movement and sound nearby generated in him an instinctive reaction to flee. His senses became fine-tuned to ensure his protection and survival.

To avoid people, Dismas began to roam the quieter parts of the city. Mostly the areas where there were more houses, away from the crowds of the markets, the theatres and the temple that dominated the city with its glaringly white marble, adorned with gold.

Being small, the narrow alleyways became helpful escape routes for him, normally ignored by others. They created a network of passages connecting the main city streets, only frequented by scavengers, the rats, dogs and small children, occasionally visited by one of the city's many petty criminals, trying to evade the attentions of the authorities.

There was a constant danger in the city from the soldiers. From an early age when out with his aunt, he had learned to fear them, to jump well out of their way as they approached. The Romans had priority on the streets and would simply push aside or even trample anyone who got in front of them. He was always aware when they were near. From streets away he could hear their armour and weapons clattering in time to their marching and would be well out of sight by the time they came by.

As Dismas explored and became more familiar with the layout of the streets, the daily search for water became easier. He discovered the system of aqueducts that supplied the city, built to carry water to quench the thirst of the wealthy in their temples and palaces. Even the palace garden had its own dedicated aqueduct to keep it looking green and healthy. Some sections were slightly elevated and provided him with a safer place to drink, not overlooked by houses. He learned the best time to visit was either at dawn or dusk when, for a few precious moments, he could relax and enjoy a rare moment of safety.

Early morning was his favourite time, just as dawn was coming and the sky started to lighten, before the sun appeared. This was his call to get up and drink. He would love to stare at the beauty of the soft colours of the sky as he took his first refreshing gulps of the day, water that would have to last him until at least sundown, or possibly until the same time the following morning.

In the springtime, he would enjoy the early morning light as it kissed the soft white and pink flowers of the tamarisk trees in the courtyards below. Across the valleys beyond the city walls, they would glow in the warm sunlight, against the dusty brown backdrop. His nostrils would fill with the sweet scent of the honeysuckles that would ramble over walls. It was a heavenly smell. Despite his wretched and lonely existence, this rare glimpse of beauty could still stir his heart, a small reminder that he was human. These trees, that looked like they were glowing, brought him a brief reprieve, a sense of peace and calm inside.

But he knew to quickly bring himself back into his reality. During those first few months on the streets Dismas learned that allowing any feelings was a dangerous luxury that he could rarely afford. Anything that reminded him of his humanity could make him want to cry. Crying would make him feel weak and he would force himself to rapidly blink away the impending tears. He must not cry. He had to be strong to survive.

Everyone hates me, so I have to hate them too. He needed to convince himself that he was alone, that people were a danger and he needed to avoid them. After taking the water he needed from the aqueduct, he would stand up tall, look around to check that no one was able to watch, and urinate into the water. If the people of Jerusalem hated him then this was one way he could get his own back on them. This simple act of defiance made him feel, for a brief moment, just a little in control over his own destiny.

After searching out water, the quest for food soon became his second obsession, as the pain in his empty stomach would almost be unbearable. He had no choice but to live on the small amounts of stolen food or scraps that he could salvage. Very few days would provide him with enough.

Dismas learned to be resourceful, discovering where there may be food at set times of the day. Jerusalem had a lot of habits and he became expert at knowing where to go and at which times, to get the most from the city's routines.

Many animals were fed better than the street children, so he would steal animal food from a trough or sack, grabbing a small handful whilst running past. Occasionally he would sneak into a stable if he spotted that the door was left ajar. When the animals were out it meant their owners were out too, and there were usually a few kernels fallen to the floor from the animals' mouths.

Another regular source of food was the street itself. At the end of the day, after the evening's cooking and eating had been completed, houses would wash their pots, ready for use again the next day. There were a few regulars that he found who would rinse out the cooking pots and hurl the water out of the door into the alleyway. He would scamper out of the shadows to join the rats in their role of cleaning the city streets, maybe gleaning a few lentils or occasionally a morsel of vegetable or meat.

To him the food markets looked like a paradise. Dismas kept away to start with, fearful of the crowds, only observing from the distant shadows. He had seen other street children venture out into the open at the market, driven to taking risks by the vision of the mountains of food on each stall. But the stallholders were sharp-eyed and observed everyone, even those who moved in the shadows nearby. They were merciless in their punishments, most keeping a long stick within their reach to beat anyone trying to steal from them. This was street justice, handed down brutally to anyone who crossed them.

He had once seen another young child tempted out of an alleyway into the marketplace. He watched as the child skulked around the back of a fruit stall, clearly desperate for food. Dismas knew what would happen. As the child reached up to take an apricot, the stallholder grabbed a stick and screamed out, 'No you don't. Get away from here!'

With full force, the stick connected with the child's shoulder, the crack of a bone breaking clearly audible. The child squealed loudly and raced back to the alley, whimpering, with his arm hanging limply by his side. Two days later Dismas saw that same child's small body lying in the gutter, rats in attendance.

It was easy to see how the colour and smells of the marketplace were so tempting for the street children. Fruits, nuts and vegetables, meats and fish all arrived daily in the markets, brought in along the city streets. Dismas developed a heightened sense of smell and could easily discern what was being carried on each cart that rattled along the cobbles, on the way to set up for a day's trading.

There were richer pickings at the end of the day in the marketplaces, immediately after the stalls had packed up for the day. There may be a few nuts or dates dropped to the ground, or a peach thrown into the gutter, too bruised to be sold, discarded in the dirt. But where there was food, there was danger too. All the street children knew what happened at the markets and the older ones would pull rank. The competition was tough and the younger ones would be risking everything to get involved.

Whilst the older street children would fight over the fallen fruit and vegetables, the grain stalls were the domain of the younger children. Dismas became adept at scurrying out at the end of the day, to where the traders had been, competing with the other younger children and the sparrows to snatch any fallen grains from the ground. Within a few minutes the marketplace was cleaned by the scavengers, ready for the next day's trading.

He became opportunistic, developing a range of strategies to help him survive. From his shadows, he would watch people wander through the market stalls towards the traders selling pistachio nuts. These then became his target. As the buyers walked away eating them, the nuts were easily dropped. Occasionally he would get a whole one but more often he would be able to follow behind, collecting the discarded shells to suck out whatever goodness and saltiness was left in them.

When the hunger pains got too much, he would resort to chewing on the mustard plants that could be found growing wild on some of the small, abandoned patches of land. The desperately bitter taste would make him feel sick, but it gave a little nourishment that would briefly quell the deep emptiness in his belly.

In the southern part of the city, it was not unusual for Dismas to scavenge from the carts on their way out through the Dung Gate towards Gehenna, that part of Jerusalem that was known as the 'living hell'. Anyone getting close to the gates in that part of the city would have the stench remaining in their nostrils for days, as the fires burned continuously, devouring the city's waste. These piles of rubbish in the valley were beyond his reach, as it would have meant going through the gates, into the open. That was the domain of the stray dogs and rats to pick through, leaving him to hone his skills of darting out into the street to grab scraps from a moving cart on its way to the dump. Occasionally his plunder was edible.

On rare occasions, Dismas would experience the kindness of strangers. If they happened to notice him and take pity on him, a coin or a cake of bread would be tossed in his direction. He could not smile, or even make eye contact with them. He would just grab the gift and run back into the shadows like a sewer rat. He could not feel gratitude, only anger, as it reminded him of his desperate situation. He would be jealous of those who had donated it to him. The rich, who had it all. The injustice would eat away at him.

A gift of food was better than a coin. Any food would be quickly eaten but a coin brought consequences. Nothing on the streets went unnoticed and the other street children, older ones, would have seen. Unless he was quick to hide away, he would be followed, beaten and robbed.

In his first two or three years of living all alone on the streets of Jerusalem, Dismas became expert at hiding away, living an unnoticed existence. He blended in, never drew any attention to himself. Anonymity became an integral part of his character.

He would go for weeks, maybe months, without speaking a word to anyone else, his existence being void of any relationships. This life had beaten out of him any sense of value. He quickly believed, deep inside, that he was worth nothing.

It became easy for him to be invisible, lost in the busyness and chaos of Jerusalem. It could happen to anyone in the blink of an eye. Outside the temple courts, he once witnessed a child wandering around, calling out 'Abba, Abba', the calls drowned out by the noise of the city. The child was panicking, tears on his cheeks, not able to see his father, lost amongst the crowds, not knowing which way to turn. Dismas could see the fear rising as the child became more distressed, but did nothing to help. He just watched.

After a few minutes, a man came running through the crowd, searching left and right, calling out a name in desperation. Dismas looked on as the man spotted his son in the crowd, raced towards him and swept him up in an embrace, kissing the boy's head, tears rolling down the father's cheeks too.

'My Immar, I thought I had lost you. I have found you. Thank you, God, he is safe. You are safe, son.'

Watching this scene, Dismas tried not to allow any feelings to penetrate the stone wall he had built around his emotions.

His was a feral existence, living life in the city's shadows, avoiding being seen in the light, as though daylight was a curse. If he ventured into the light, into view, he was likely to be shouted at, possibly chased away. If he were to be caught it could lead to a beating, injury, or worse.

Exposure to the light was perilous, but darkness also brought many dangers. Dismas became adept at picking those moments of the day when it was just light enough to see what he was doing, but not so dark that he would be left endangered. As darkness embraced the city, it was a time to hide away and keep an even lower profile.

The city was black at night, with a beam of light only occasionally shining into the streets through open doorways, or from a Roman patrol with torches lighting their way. In the blackness lurked danger. There were stories of men who would scout around the city streets at night, looking for children. These men were to be avoided. Children would disappear, no doubt to be sold as slaves.

The city walls were safe at night, deserted. When the night air was too cold to stay still for any length of time, Dismas took to walking along quiet sections of the wall. He learned to be so light on his feet that he could move around without making any sound, his silent footsteps unnoticed. Up on the walls he could stand tall, scanning the distant horizons, dreaming of what life beyond the walls might be like. He could see fires on hillsides and valleys in the distance, probably shepherds warning off wolves and keeping themselves warm. He longed to be able to stand in front of a fire and feel its warmth.

During the busy festivals, when the roads approaching the city were lined with the tents of the visiting pilgrims, from the top of the walls he could see a line of flickering lamps and fires snaking away from the city. The smoke would rise and the breeze would waft the smells of their exotic cooking. In the evenings the noise would be constant from the donkeys and camels, the shouting, singing and laughing of the travellers, reminding him of the celebrations that he was excluded from. Or in the dead of night the sound of a baby crying would cut through the silence as it drifted across the valley to Dismas, waiting and watching at the top of the city wall.

Occasionally, from out of the blackness, the sound of a wolf would carry on the wind from across the hills. Or owls, those birds the adults used to tell young children scary stories about, could be heard screeching and hooting from out of the darkness. And dogs barking, always, right through the night. City dogs setting each other off in a chain reaction from house to house, or wild dogs outside the walls, especially after there had been a crucifixion. On a still night they could be heard fighting and tearing at the bodies that the Romans had left hanging on the crosses overnight. At dawn they would be joined by a frenzy of buzzards and vultures, as they devoured the remnants of the previous day's victims.

Dismas would enjoy a bright full moon, the only friendly face he would allow to break through the veneer of solitude that now shrouded his life. It would bring a modicum of safety to the dark streets at night. And the stars, a mystery to him, like a brief glimpse of heaven bringing a little hope to his life. But on these clear nights the air would be too cold for him to ponder for very long. He had no cloak to wrap himself in and no fire to warm himself next to. He had to keep moving.

Chapter 5
A Sweet Fragrance

How delightful is your love, my sister, my bride! How much more pleasing is your love than wine, and the fragrance of your perfume more than any spice! (Song of Songs 4:10)

For Dismas to survive it was imperative for him to be cautious of everyone. There was no moral code on the streets. He knew of plenty of street children who would not hesitate to beat or even kill others, just for a mouthful of food. There was a small group at the top of the pecking order who were known to have knives. They were to be avoided at all costs. To them, life was cheap.

Dismas had witnessed a gang arguing over something, food probably. In the midst of the shouting and shoving, the leader drew his knife and lunged at one of the other boys, plunging it into his stomach. When he pulled his arm back, the victim clutched his blood-stained tunic, making a gurgling noise that made Dismas retch. The whole gang scattered without looking back, leaving the stabbed boy to collapse to the ground, deserted and abandoned in death. Life destroyed in an instant, without a care from anyone.

Genuine friendships were rare and no one was to be trusted. It was a lonely existence, but it had to be if he wanted to stay alive.

There was only one person that Dismas ever learnt to trust. He was never quite sure how or why it happened, but he became friends with a girl called Riha. He first saw her one evening, hugging the shadows on the other side of the street from where he was skulking. She was perhaps the same age as him, thin and bony, straggly straight black hair to her shoulders, barefoot and dirty, the same as all street children. Her dark red tunic was stained and torn. He did not take much notice of her; she was just another child fighting for the same scraps as him.

Early the next morning, still in the same part of town, he was crouched in the shadows, watching the day unfold, when she darted around the corner from the street and jumped into the alleyway beside him. Dismas froze with fear. The two of them looked at each other, both surprised and nervous of how the other may react. This sort of close contact with anyone else was rare for him and dangerous for them both.

A nervous smile flashed across Riha's face, causing small dimples to form in her cheeks, which seemed to disarm the situation. Dismas must have responded with a look or some body language showing a small encouragement to her, because she relaxed and crouched down next to him. The anxiety subsided.

'Hello,' she said in a whisper. Dismas just looked at her.

'I saw you here yesterday from across the street,' she added. 'My name is Riha.' A bit more confidence was creeping into her words.

Dismas stared at her, remaining completely motionless like a terrified animal. There was an accent to her voice, like many of the pilgrim visitors to the city. Riha was a name he knew. It meant 'perfume, a sweet fragrance'. He thought to himself that this could not be further from the truth.

'Do you have a name?'

Dismas hesitated.

'Yes,' he eventually managed to say.

She looked at him with an amused look on her face.

'Are you going to tell me what it is?' A soft smile appeared, as though she understood a joke he was having with her. Dismas could not see why anything was funny.

His eyes darted towards the street, which was getting busier as the morning trade picked up. It was not safe to run now. He was going to have to stay here.

Nervously he said, 'Dismas,' and he looked down to the ground. He feared the pattern of this conversation, what her next words would be and the memories and shame that would come flooding back into his mind.

'I like that name,' came the happy reply. And that was it. It took a few moments of silence for Dismas' shame to dive back down, to be hidden deep inside again.

The morning passed with the two of them hidden away together. Riha would whisper the occasional comment or observation; Dismas would listen but offer no response. As the heat rose towards the middle of the day, the streets began to quieten down and Dismas was thinking that his time to escape from her would be soon.

'Look,' Riha said in a loud, excited whisper that broke their silence. She nodded her head towards an older lady who was waddling slowly along the street towards them, with a basket in each arm, each a little too full of provisions. They both knew that she was an easy target. She had no free arm to take a swipe at them.

'You take the left basket and I'll take the right one.'

Panic rose inside him again. The risk was more than he would normally take.

'I'm not sure,' he stuttered.

'This is an easy one. I have seen you run. You are fast like me. We can get food from this one.' Riha was full of confidence.

Dismas had no idea how to say no. While he fought the internal battle as to whether he should join in or not, the lady had already walked past the entrance to the alleyway.

'Are you ready?'

Dismas just looked at her, his face covered in panic.

'Go!' and before he had the chance to think twice, Dismas found he was scurrying out from the shadows alongside Riha, into the street. There was a sudden change in temperature as he launched from the shade into the strong sunlight. He squinted in the brightness and his heart was beating fast. Approaching the woman from behind would give them the element of surprise. She never saw them coming. They raced up to her and, before she knew what was happening, each of them had grabbed a basket. A few steps further on and Riha darted left into the next alley. Dismas followed close behind, leaving behind him the weak shouts from the old lady. The two of them kept on running to the end, Riha in front. After a short pause to check it was clear, they scampered across the next street into another alley. They had escaped into the shadows of the city, stopping only when they were sure that no one was following.

The two of them were breathing heavily as the adrenalin pumped through their veins. For both of them this was more than just survival. It was exhilarating.

'That was amazing,' she squealed excitedly. 'I told you that you were fast.'

Dismas allowed himself a brief secret smile.

'Let's look in the baskets,' she said, but Dismas could only look at her suspiciously. She could tell what he was thinking.

'Don't worry, I am not going to run off. This is for us to share. I promise.'

He watched her closely as she peered into the basket she was holding. He was going to let her go first, in case this was a trick. His hands tightened their grip on his basket. She pulled out some flat bread, dried fruit, nuts and olive oil. As his trust built, he delved into his basket and found more bread, and best of all there were four fresh peaches. Dismas had never had such a good harvest.

They squatted down in a quiet corner and shared this feast with each other. They gorged on the bread, dried fruit and nuts until their stomachs hurt. But they still had room to eat two peaches each. They shared the pleasure of eating that sweet peach flesh, the juice covering their hands and faces.

As they slumped back with full stomachs and satisfied smiles, he watched Riha pour some of the oil into her cupped hand and rub it into the skin on her hands and arms. She then took some more in her hands and began to massage it into her face. The scent of the oil filled the air around them, reminding him of his aunt's and uncle's home where the oil lamps would burn all day long, leaving a permanent infusion of oil through the whole house. Dismas could only stare at her. She really was a sweet fragrance. He allowed himself to think, for a few brief seconds, that he was making a friend.

From that moment, it seemed natural to both of them to be alongside each other. Dismas and Riha became inseparable. He did not speak much and she was quite accepting of this. They exchanged the occasional smile as Dismas slowly became more comfortable making eye contact with her. She had found someone who was no threat to her in any way. They worked well together, finding that two pairs of eyes and ears made life safer. They were comfortable sharing the same space and looking out for each other.

Riha was used to roaming a different patch of the city, which she introduced to Dismas. She took him to places he was not familiar with and had been too scared to go into. They ventured onto the cobbled streets of the upper city, the more lively parts of Jerusalem near the theatre. They would dream about what lay inside the white marble mansions and large palaces.

The city walls were still their boundary, too frightened to venture into the world beyond. Whenever she saw one of the gates, Riha would wonder out loud, chattering about what life outside must be like.

'I heard people say there is so much food there. They call it a land full of milk and honey. There are forests with trees taller than the temple and mountains so high they have white snow on the top of them. Rivers and lakes so you can stay clean. Someone told me there is an ocean with so much water you can't even see over to the other side. Food enough for everyone. Beautiful robes to wear. Flowers and fruit and perfumes. It must be like heaven. We should go one day.'

But they both knew that this was only a dream. It would never happen.

The bazaars in the upper city were less crowded and to Dismas they were not as good, but he never told her this. Riha suggested where they would go each morning and he simply followed like a faithful puppy.

Riha would chatter with excitement as they watched the Xystus market, her voice barely audible over the sound of the constant bartering, shouting and haggling. Its colonnades offered more variation than those in the lower city. Daily baked bread, fish, honey, wines and animal skins all brought a variety of new smells, permanently mixed with the strong scent of crushed olives. The colour came from the trinkets, pots and the fabric stalls displaying rolls of cloth from all over the world. Silks, velvets and fine linens that Riha loved to stare at, as she dreamed of wearing clothes made from such beautiful colours.

When they saw a wedding procession passing through the streets one day, Riha was talking about it for days afterwards.

'The bride looked so beautiful, didn't she? Did you see her colourful clothes? Did you see her jewellery and the crown on the bridegroom's head?

'You know they carry her in that litter all the way to the bridegroom's house and then there is a huge party, with singing and dancing and celebrating for days.'

When Riha had started to sing along to their celebrations, twirling and skipping to the tune, she sang out, 'Join in!'

But Dismas could not feel the joy. He was not able to sing or dance.

Then she said with all seriousness, 'I am going to go to a wedding one day.'

She loved seeing the animals, too, that were plentiful around the temple. Lambs, goats, doves, chickens all brought colour, noise and chaos to the atmosphere. They would see the bulls being driven through the streets in the early morning, the deep rumbling of their hooves bringing a sense of their own impending doom at the hands of the priests.

'I think it's cruel!' she would say indignantly, when she saw pilgrims buying the animals to then hand them over to the priests simply to sacrifice. 'It's not fair! Why should the animals have to die? And why should God get all this food when we have none?'

At busy times of the year like Passover, there would be an overpowering smell of blood emanating from the temple courtyard. The stench would make her angry. The black smoke would lurk menacingly over the temple courts, a north-east breeze would fill the city streets with the scent of burning lamb.

They were creeping alongside a wall one grey morning, adjacent to where a market was being set up for the day, when the very opportunity she had been looking for presented itself. A trader was setting up his tables, whilst his animals, in their baskets and cages, were still on the cart behind him.

'Look!' Riha whispered. 'This is our chance.'

'Chance for what?' All he could see were the animals, which were no good to them.

'I'm going to set them free,' she declared.

Dismas could not understand why this was important, or worth taking a risk for. But she had that look of determination on her face which he knew he was never going to change.

'You wait here for me,' he was instructed.

He did as he was told and watched her creep along the shadow of the wall and dive unnoticed under the cart. She popped her head up in the gap between the cart and the wall, reached over and began to undo the cages and baskets holding the birds. As the lids were flipped open, Dismas could see the chickens lift their heads, perplexed at what was happening. The doves were a little cleverer, hopping up to the edge of the baskets, looking up to the rooftops to survey their escape routes.

Riha had a look of pure joy on her face. With as many baskets open as she could reach, she began overturning them, flailing her arms around, shooing the birds away, freeing them from their captivity. The cart became a turmoil of clucking, squealing, flapping, only made more chaotic when the trader turned around to see his birds escaping. He began to race around, chasing chickens that were evading him in every direction. All the doves rose from the cart in unison, encircling the scene, leaving only a few white feathers spiralling down towards the empty baskets.

Onlookers were revelling in this comical show, pointing and laughing at the man chasing the chickens that were determined not to be caught.

Riha scurried back beside Dismas, breathing hard.

'Look at him trying to catch those chickens!' She laughed excitedly. 'And look at the doves up there, on the roofs. They're free. That was so good!'

Dismas found it hard to see why, but was glad it had made her happy.

During feasts and festivals there would be many of these temporary booths along the main roads leading to the temple. The thousands of visitors to the city from all over the country, and from other countries, did not want to miss this opportunity to bring their merchandise to trade with the crowds. Plus the city needed a lot of extra food to cater for the huge celebrations that they all enjoyed. Jerusalem would be busier and noisier than usual, with plenty of laughter and music filling the streets in the evenings. This only made them feel even more separated, rejected and outcast by the city, excluded from its festivities.

One chilly morning, the city was preparing for Hanukkah, the Festival of Lights. Riha noticed the stalls selling candles and oil setting up in the streets.

'It must be my birthday soon,' she said casually. 'I was born around festival time. When's your birthday?'

This most innocent of questions triggered the deep pain, which rose up from his core. The hurt and rejection of his uncle's words flashed into his mind and haunted him. He could only look at the ground and mumble, 'I don't know.' And he was overcome with embarrassment.

He had no idea at all when his birthday was, or even how old he was. He thought he could be ten or eleven years old, but he had never learned how to gauge the time of the year or bothered to count the seasons or festivals that the city celebrated. Inside he vowed that from now on he would start to take notice.

When he looked up from his shame, he saw Riha gazing at him with tears in her eyes. She understood. He could only cast his eyes back down at the ground. Neither of them had any words. She looked down at his hand and took hold of it, grasping it tightly. Dismas had no idea how to react or what to say, feeling so uncomfortable with her expression of emotion. He just let it happen.

As they stood there together, hand in hand, for the first time in many years Dismas dared to think that someone genuinely cared for him. But he had no ability or intention of letting this weakness show. It could only lead to disappointment.

'I know,' she chirped after a few minutes, trying to be more cheerful. 'You can have my birthday. We can celebrate your birthday on the same day as me. We can be twins.'

They shared a nervous smile and it was agreed.

'We'll do it tomorrow.'

That night they sheltered in an out-building, not far from the Valley Gate in the east of the city, being as still and quiet as they could so as not to disturb the chickens that were sharing their stall. It was a clear, cold night. Through the gaps in the thatch roof they could see the stars glittering high above them, all the more vibrant for the lack of moon. They needed each other that night, to avoid freezing to death, curled up next to each other like two young mice in a nest. It was a rare occasion that they felt safe and for a few hours they could sleep soundly.

Before dawn, Riha sat up and shook his shoulder.

'Wake up!' the breath from her loud whisper misted in the cold. It never took much effort to wake up when one ear was always alert to any sound of danger. 'It is time to go.'

'Where to?' Dismas asked. 'It is too early for anything.'

'It's our birthday! And I have a gift for you.'

Dismas was wide eyed. He had never had a birthday before, or a gift. They gathered themselves together and crept out of the door, doing all they could to avoid any sound that might wake a nearby sleeping dog. Once in the street, he followed her through the darkness as she guided them towards the city walls. She led him to some steps that went up to the top of the walls and they scampered up.

When they reached the top, Riha announced, 'This is it. Let's sit down here,' and the two of them sat down looking out towards the east. They sat close to ward off the chill and Riha took his hand again. He had no urge to pull it away.

The silence was broken by the cautious beginnings of the dawn chorus. The birdsong rose from the land below them, announcing the new day with a joy that he had never noticed before.

'The only gift I could think of for your birthday was this,' whispered Riha. They looked out across the Kidron Valley in front of them. 'I want to give you the sky.'

The scene in front of them was transforming in the emerging light. The bright stars were fading as the sun began to shed its light from far beyond the horizon. The sky changed from black, to dark blue, then lighter blues mixed with the yellows, pinks and purples as the early morning sunlight refracted off the few wisps of high-up cloud.

As the sun broke through the horizon, the stone and dust in the valley glowed orange. The dew on the olive and tamarisk trees, glinting gold and silver in the light, began to rise on the sunlight as whisps of mist. These delicate veils of mist, glowing orange and pink, drifted along the valley floor and then melted away under the early morning sun. It was beautiful and serene, disturbed only by the occasional goat bleating on the opposite hillside, or a cockerel announcing the coming day.

It was the most wonderful sight Dismas had ever seen. He had rarely been able to see any beauty in creation. He sat there, mesmerised by the colours changing in front of them.

'I like this.'

She responded with a broad smile and a gentle squeeze of his hand.

'But I don't have anything to give to you,' he suddenly felt guilty that he had not even thought about a gift.

'Don't worry. This is our birthday. We share everything today, so this is a gift for both of us.'

He was happy with that.

They watched together as a pair of eagles rose from the crags on the opposite hillside. These majestic birds fanned out their wings and tails and began to rise on the warming air, soaring ever higher above the vineyards in the valley. The children could only dream about that sort of freedom, to be able to fly away from all of this, to escape their incarceration. Dismas felt her hand tighten around his as they both held on to the same dreams.

As the morning grew lighter it became more dangerous for them to stay on top of the wall. They soaked in one last look and then sloped away. The remainder of their birthday was a normal, uneventful day of finding water, hiding away, scavenging for food and trying to stay warm and dry.

But it had been the most special day of his life.

Chapter 6
Hope Destroyed

*Even though I walk through the valley of the shadow of death,
I will fear no evil, for you are with me; your rod and your staff,
they comfort me.* (Psalm 23:4)

That winter seemed long, making their Hanukkah birthday celebration soon feel like a distant memory. It was especially cold and wet that season. For weeks they could never dry out or get warm. The mud caked their feet and legs, which gave them a scent they could not shake off. Unless they were continually moving, their damp bodies would shiver constantly.

Sabbath days were always more difficult. There were no markets, so food was limited and hunger pangs were worse. The poor were forgotten on the sabbath, further fuelling Dismas' view that the religious people were the worst. They often did the opposite of what they preached.

A risk worth taking on the sabbath was to sneak inside the temple courts, to hide amongst the crowds and grab some fresh bread from one of the stalls. On a sabbath day, their punishment would be nothing worse than getting thrown out of the temple courts. The temple guards were astute, efficient and to be avoided, but even they were not allowed to beat children on a sabbath. It was usual for the guards to spot and evict any street children fairly swiftly. Nothing that filthy and impure was allowed to encroach so close to their God.

One damp and grey sabbath, Dismas and Riha sneaked through the gates into the temple outer courts and were lurking in the darkness of Solomon's Colonnade. All around them was the usual noise from men praying out loud, preaching to the crowds from the steps, or small gatherings arguing about why their beliefs were right. Often the preaching would turn into shouting or scuffles, as disagreements broke out over the finer details of their religious laws. All of them convinced that they spoke the truth and the words they had to share were the most important for everyone to hear.

The two children had managed to glean a small cake of bread and were squatting against a cold column of stone, eating. From nowhere, a hand shot out and grabbed Riha, holding her tight at the top of her arm.

'Got you!' and the guard looked pleased with himself. A temple guard had spotted her and she was caught. Dismas pulled back around the column so he could not be seen. He was safe, but fearful of what could happen to her.

The normal pattern would be to follow her to the gate, where she would be thrown out with a few harsh words. But he saw a different scene unfolding that filled him with panic. The guard, holding her tightly despite her struggles, marched her to the edge of the Colonnade. When he reached the top step he paused and looked out across the court, where only a few people were milling around. He caught the eye of a man who was on the opposite side and gave him a subtle nod. Dismas knew instinctively what was going on. The guard was handing her over.

The man was shrouded in a dark mantle that wrapped around him, with a hood pulled up over his head. Where his face should have been there was just darkness. He quickly marched across the court towards the foot of the steps. Riha, still trying to squirm free, saw the man approaching and let out a shriek.

'No!' she screamed out. 'Don't give me to him!' But no one seemed to take much notice. The guard's grip tightened on her arms. He might get a good pay-out for this one.

Dismas had to think fast. He darted out behind the guard and kicked him on the back of the knee with all the force he could muster. The guard's leg buckled and he howled. For a brief second, he released his grip and Riha broke free. The two of them instinctively ran as fast as they could. They darted through the crowds unnoticed and raced through the temple gates into the cover of the city.

They ran until they were well out of sight of the temple, finding shelter in the safety of an alleyway. Riha was terrified, tears rolling down her cheeks, her eyes full of fear.

'That was too close,' she sobbed between breaths. 'I saw that man coming over. He was going to hand me over. I've seen men like him around before. They sell children as slaves. I was warned never to go near those sorts of men. I nearly got taken.'

After a few minutes she calmed down. She looked at Dismas.

'You saved me. Thank you.'

Dismas just looked down at his feet, a little embarrassed.

'No, I mean it,' she insisted. 'Look at me.' Dismas looked up at her.

'You saved my life. Thank you.'

He smiled and looked away again. He felt proud of what he had done. It was the bravest he had ever been and he was so pleased with himself for protecting her.

The rest of that day they stayed hidden away, no appetite for any sort of adventure. They were exhausted and thoughtful about what may have been.

In the early evening, as light was fading, Riha inspected her injuries. There was dark grey bruising around her upper arms where the guard had been holding her tight. She broke their silence.

'Dismas, you have never told me why you are here.'

Dismas just shrugged. He did not want to talk about it.

'I know you don't like talking. I am glad you are here though. If you hadn't been here, I would probably be a slave by now.'

The words hung heavily in the air.

They were both thinking the same thoughts. Their reality was not that much better than slavery. Neither of them wanted to voice it, but they knew that she may have been better off if she had been taken.

Dismas had never honestly pondered his own situation before now. *Why am I still here? Would going back home be any worse than this?* He had convinced himself that he was better off on the streets, independent and free from the torment and abuse. But there was a high price to pay for freedom. Perhaps the harsh truth was that he had no real freedom now. It was fear, pride and shame that was keeping him from returning to his aunt and uncle.

*

Every cloak, blanket or rag became a prized possession. Late one afternoon, Dismas had passed a half-open doorway to a mikvah, one of many across this city to serve a people who were obsessed with getting clean. It was rare for the doors to be left open, especially when it was cold, so he took notice. This one must have been left off its latch and blown open. He cautiously peered inside and could hear the low murmurs of men talking, punctuated by the splashing from their ceremonial washings. And there on a bench in front of him, near the door, were the men's clothes.

His actions took no thought or planning. Instinctively he dived in, grabbed at a pile of clothes and ran away as fast as he could. Even before he got back to Riha, he was inwardly excited about what he may have got for them. *I am sure this will please her.* To his delight, she was thrilled as they examined his haul. There was a man's tunic, white with short sleeves; a head covering which was simply a white square of linen; and a heavy dark-brown cloak, made of wool.

'You have the tunic,' insisted Riha. 'Put it on over the top of your clothes.'

Dismas put it on and it came down to his ankles, which brought them both out in giggles. Riha then took the head covering and wrapped it around her head. She pranced around pretending to be one of the religious men they would see striding around the city, which made them both laugh some more. She took it and wrapped it over her shoulders like a shawl.

'The cloak we can share,' she said. 'And can you imagine the look on that man's face when he found his clothes had gone. He would have had to walk home with nothing on!' and they laughed again. 'Well, we need these more than he does.'

As night came, they settled down, huddled together under the new cloak, for once warm.

Something woke Dismas in the darkest hours of the night. The cloak was being whipped off them and disappeared into the darkness before he could grab at it. Someone had crept up on them and stolen it away, leaving them again exposed to the cold night air. This sort of thing was just a part of their life on the streets. Riha had not woken and he thought nothing more of it. He tried to settle and sleep a little more, but it was cold and he was shivering again.

Their usual routine would be to wake at dawn, before heading off to find water. But on that cold morning, when Dismas and Riha were sheltering next to each other in a dirty alleyway, Riha, usually bright and lively, was instead lethargic and difficult to wake. Her gentle groans sent a panic through Dismas, telling him that something was not right.

Disease was a constant threat for anyone in the city, with the fear of a plague often at the top of the list for gossipers around the markets. For children on the street it was worse, with the threat of disease and infection heightened by the risks from what they ate, insect bites or just due to the lack of any hygiene. Even the vermin on the streets were a danger; the rats and dogs could creep up to gnaw on a sleeping child at night.

Dismas felt her forehead and knew she was full of fever. She was shivering in the cold of the morning, despite droplets of sweat on her brow and her skin feeling so hot. Her face was grey and her lips were dry and cracked.

He tried to wake her, but she was drowsy.

'Do you need a drink?' and she gave a slight nod of her head.

His mind was confused and filled with dread. He tucked her clothes in tight to her body to try to keep her warm and left to fetch water. As he raced through the back alleys to the nearest aqueduct, the horror began to overwhelm him. He was filled with fear.

He scoured the doorways of a few nearby houses and quickly spotted a small jar just inside an entrance. He silently grabbed it and headed for the water. It was a round trip of about an hour and when he returned there was no change in her condition. He lifted her head up and gently put the water to her lips. She took a few small mouthfuls and sank limply back down.

He sat with her through the day. She mostly slept, so he kept alert, hoping that nothing would disturb them. She would hardly be able to move or run away. His head was in turmoil thinking about what he would have to do if they were discovered. *I can't run and abandon her. Would I be able to stand and protect her?*

When it got to late afternoon he knew she needed food, so he ventured out again. He did not want to go far. She was in danger, alone and ill, unable to escape. He took a risk by stealing some bread from a trader when there were fewer crowds around to give him cover, but he got away with it. He raced back to Riha who, to his relief, was still there.

She ate a little and took some more water.

'Thank you,' she whispered to him as she tried to raise a smile.

Darkness fell and the cold crept in again. How they needed that cloak tonight.

Dismas took off his new tunic and laid it over Riha, in a futile attempt to keep her warm. He lay as close to her as he could, to offer warmth and protection, but the two of them still shivered through the night. Dismas did not sleep at all, as fear enveloped him like the darkness all around.

At dawn, he sat up when she stirred. He looked at her and could tell she was worse. Her eyes were empty with dark rings around them. Her face was devoid of all colour. He encouraged her to take a little more water, but she could not manage any scraps of the hard, stale bread.

Throughout the morning she was in and out of consciousness. When she slept, she was breathing so lightly that he worried she was dead. When she was awake and had her eyes open, all he could see in her face was sadness and fear, and he wanted her to be asleep again. He felt helpless, unable to muster any words of comfort. He sat with her all that time, sometimes holding her listless hand and gently stroking the hair on the side of her head. The turmoil inside him was intense. His helplessness was devouring him. He did not know what to say or do to save her.

Later in the afternoon, for just half an hour the sun would touch the dark alleyway where they were hiding. The warmth seeped into them both and for a few moments she stirred. She took a little more water and tried to speak, but could not manage any words. He looked into her eyes and he saw tears forming. They both knew what was coming.

The brief warmth from the sun departed and he lay down next to her, helpless and hopeless. He rested his head on her chest. With one ear he could hear her heart beating away quickly, and with the other ear he could hear her shallow breaths. As nightfall approached, she let out a quiet moan with her last breath. He heard a beat of her heart and then silence. No more. That silence destroyed him. It drained him of all hope.

As the sun disappeared, light departed from the alleyway and life left her fragile body.

*

Dismas was paralysed with grief. For hours he could not move, plunged into darkness and lost in his own abandonment. The void inside of him was growing.

He felt a sense of duty to stand guard over her precious body, to protect it from the scurrying scavengers that were encircling this wretched scene. They could smell death. He would not let them take even a sniff at her. He stayed there all night, clinging on to the thin slither of respite that she had briefly brought to his pitiful existence.

At the end of that loneliest and longest night, as first light finally arrived, by her side he found the remnants of the olive oil that she had treasured from that day they first met. He took the stopper out of the bottle and carefully poured it over her forehead. As the few remaining drops ran down her face, he gently wiped the oil across her cheeks as though wiping away tears. The oil gave her skin a little colour as it glistened in the early morning sun.

He really wanted to say something. To tell her how much she had meant to him. That she had been a perfect companion. That she had brought him so much hope and glimpses of joy that he never thought would be possible. But he could not even open his mouth. He had no ability to express these feelings. He hated that he was so lost for words. He could only settle for his usual unsatisfactory silence.

Dismas had just a few moments now before the streets got too busy. He did not have the strength to lift her body, so he crouched down behind her, put his hands under her arms and dragged her to the end of the alleyway. He checked quickly to see that there was no one around and as soon as it was clear he moved her into the street. He carefully sat her in the gutter opposite, slumped against the wall of a house, leaning forwards with her shoulders and face bent down to the ground. Here her body would be safe from the rodent scavengers that also dared not be seen in the street in the daylight. As the city awoke, he knew her body would be taken care of.

He watched from the shadows of the alleyway opposite. As expected, an early patrol of Roman soldiers came past and spotted the corpse. They took a closer look, kicked the body and got no reaction. They were reluctant to get too close at the risk of catching whatever disease may have killed her, or wary of the fleas and lice that it may spread.

They moved on, and for about an hour the city's early risers simply stepped around or over the body as it lay there, no one showing any interest. Then a cart arrived. As expected, the soldiers had reported it. The man stepped down and prodded the body with his foot, just to make sure. He took a shroud from his cart and threw it loosely over her, so that he would not have to touch death. He had no trouble lifting her limp body and placing it onto the cart.

Riha was gone. His uncle's words came to his mind . . . Riha had been returned to the dust. She came from the dust, lived in the dust and was now returning to the dust.

Dismas could not move, lost in a quagmire of thoughts and regrets. He realised he knew nothing about her. *Where was she from? How did she end up living on the streets?* He had never been capable of asking. He did not know if she had ever had a family. His guilt grew into self-hatred, loathing himself for his failure to care for her properly.

The following days and weeks were desperate. Dismas felt more deserted and alone than ever. He had no motivation to eat or even seek warmth. The instincts for survival that he had developed had been beaten into submission by a deep loss and an ever-growing anger. His hope had been shattered. Inside he raged at the unfairness of his life, the weakness he had shown in letting his guard down and getting close to someone, and even fury at Riha for leaving him alone. His anger was devouring him from the inside, whilst on the outside he just showed a blank facade.

The rains continued, turning the alleyways into stinking running sewers. The foul odour filled his nostrils and infused his rags. Fragrance had left his life and been replaced with a stench that he felt he fully deserved, affirming his place as a part of the city's waste.

Chapter 7
Into the Depths

He lifted me out of the slimy pit, out of the mud and mire; he set my feet on a rock and gave me a firm place to stand. (Psalm 40:2)

These dark memories had been pouring out of Habib. The trauma had never been far from the surface, but as the torrent of hurts and damage came flooding out from him, they were released to the light. They were dealt with. There was closure.

He could sense that Jesus was still beside him, holding him firmly by the hand, a deep and personal reassurance, like a midwife supporting a mother at the birth of a child. Jesus was silent, bringing peace and calm.

Habib, too, remained still and quiet, soaking in the peace that was overpowering his trauma. In his mind he could clearly picture Riha's dimpled face, streaked with dust, smiling warmly at him. She was the only person he could remember who ever looked at him, rather than through him. *Is she here too?*

This thought circulated around his mind and grew increasingly louder. He wanted to know if Riha was here. If he would see her again. His heart was now pounding. He wanted to ask. He had to know. Inside he was pleading to know if she was here too. He opened his mouth to ask but the words just would not come.

He opened his eyes, squinting and blinking at the immense light that was so bright, it's warmth engulfing and cleansing. As his eyes adjusted and his vision returned, he found himself face to face with Jesus.

Jesus looked deeply into his eyes and he felt a wave of reassurance overcome him. And he knew. That glint in Jesus' eye, the knowing smile and gentle nod told him what he needed to know. He knew. Riha was here. She had been rescued too. He would see her again. He need not ask the question because he knew for certain that he would be with her again.

He was now bathing in the light, so bright and warm, permeating his body. He felt truly enlightened, radiating with these new feelings of love, peace and hope that it nurtured within him.

He felt strong and equipped to continue with his story.

*

A life that had been founded on the pure instinct to survive, morphed rapidly into one that was solely an expression of the deep rage that was growing inside him. His anger began to manifest as brutal rebellion. The world had rejected him and hated him, and so he was determined to turn against the world. The streets of Jerusalem became his target.

Dismas was now alone, living every day fuelled by fear and mistrust. Fear of other street children, fear of the authorities, fear of all people, fear of the day and the night, fear of hunger and death, fear of the shame and pain that lived deep within him. Inside he felt compelled to do all he could to rid himself of the memory of Riha before it tore him apart.

He descended into the depths of despair and hopelessness. He vowed to himself that he would never get close to anyone again. It only led to pain. He was never going to talk about Riha or even think about her. It was too painful to remember what had been lost. He had to protect himself.

Life became a fog. He was numb to any feelings or any awareness of what was happening around him. There was nothing remarkable or different, just the mundane, featureless, greyness of daily survival. He led a solitary life, perhaps only speaking a handful of words each week. He did not even speak to himself.

The first year after Riha died, the Festival of Lights did spark some emotions within him as he remembered their shared birthday. But he buried them deep and it was bearable. The second time around it passed by without any recognition, blanked from his mind.

As he reached the age of twelve or thirteen, he became aware that his status on the streets may be changing. He had become one of the older children, more experienced and streetwise than the younger ones. He noticed the youngsters would cower from him when he scowled at them, if they dared to come close. He was mysterious to them, enigmatic, feared, and he liked the feeling of respect that it brought.

There were not many older boys around, whether they had died or been captured he did not know and did not care. There were a lot of younger boys and girls on the streets, but no older girls. They all disappeared.

As he became more confident of his place in the hierarchy, and less scared of the other boys, he started to feel safer spending some time in their company. He discovered that there was some benefit in working together. Being in a gang was convenient and fruitful, but in no way was there any loyalty. He would trust no one. He knew that any of them would instinctively give up on or desert another without a thought. He was still very alone.

It was on a quiet sabbath that Dismas came across a new partner. On this particular day, the temple guards had the upper hand. Dismas was once again caught taking some bread and a temple guard had him by the arms, marching him towards the exit. As they approached the temple gates, coming towards them was a mirror image, another guard holding another boy.

'You got one too, then?' said the guard holding Dismas.

They turned through the gates at the same time and the two boys were hurled down the steps together, landing in the dust, bruised but nothing broken. Behind them they could hear shouts from the guards of 'Now stay out!' and 'Don't come back.'

Dismas recognised the other boy. He had been on the streets for as long as Dismas could remember, probably a year or two older than him, and taller. They had never spoken before, but now found themselves sat in the dirt together, as worshippers stepped around them and over them on their way into the temple courts. The two boys picked themselves up and skulked over to the shelter of the nearest alleyway.

'I'm Gestas, son of Harhas.' Dismas was bemused by the arrogance, but then he had never known himself to be anyone's son. Fortunately, Gestas was not bothered or interested in any reply and Dismas was not going to willingly offer anything.

'That's our chance gone of any food today. I'm going to get some water. You coming?'

Dismas looked at him and nodded, then tailed along behind him as they headed off to the nearest aqueduct. For Dismas, this could be a way in to gain a new ally. Friendship would be a step too far, but at least a partner or acquaintance. He was cautious, but astute enough to realise that it was also better not to have enemies.

From then on, Gestas and Dismas worked the streets together as a regular partnership.

Gestas was never a pleasant character to be around. His name meant 'to complain' or 'to grumble' and he did this constantly. He was never a true friend and certainly would not think twice about stealing food or coins from Dismas or leaving him behind if they had to run. His particular pleasure was to laugh at other people's misfortune.

Just for the fun of it he would taunt the beggars and lepers. The city was plagued with the poor, the beggars sat on every street tapping their wooden bowls to attract attention. The blind, the deaf, the lame and the mute were well represented and Gestas hated them all. He saw each of them as fair targets, even if only for the sport. He would creep up on them to steal their coins, or walk closely past them as they sat in the gutter and kick them, then run away laughing.

As they walked along the street he would absent-mindedly pick up a handful of stones from the ground and hurl them at a beggar across the road. Anything to deflect the attention towards others and help him avoid having to face up to his own misfortunes. Dismas did not like this cruelty but was equally ashamed that he never did anything to intervene.

Gestas hated the Romans even more than he hated the beggars and he made no secret of how he had ended up living on the streets because of them. According to Gestas, there was an argument between his father and a patrol of Roman soldiers. His father lost his temper and attacked them, only to be killed in the street in front of him. His mother was taken off too as she clung to his father's body, howling with grief, leaving the young boy on his own on the street.

A few years on now, Gestas was taller than most children on the streets. Dressed in the typical filthy rags, his black curly hair fell down around his angular, scabby face, tangling with the fluffy beard that had started growing on his chin. He had deep-set eyes that gave little away and when he spoke, the gap from his missing front teeth was clearly visible.

His long legs meant that he was a faster runner than Dismas. He could quickly stride out from the shadows and grab whatever they had been eyeing up. Before the stallholders in the market could see him, he would be away, dodging and sidestepping through the crowd back to the shadows. Joining forces with him was convenient and mostly lucrative for Dismas.

Gestas habitually enjoyed being too fast for Dismas, to purposely cause him trouble. In front of a bread stall one morning, he decided to play a usual trick.

'You stand in front and distract him. I'll creep up from the other side and grab the bread. We'll meet up round the corner.'

They did just that. Dismas approached from one direction, in plain sight so that the stallholder would see him. The man picked up his stick and was drawn away from his stall, whilst Gestas sneaked up from the other side, grabbed a hunk of bread and ran. Only this time, instead of turning on his heel to disappear unnoticed, Gestas ran straight towards Dismas, past the stall holder, pushing him in the back as he ran past. The man howled, and after the initial shock he started after the two of them.

Dismas was so surprised that he reacted too slowly. The stallholder was bearing down on him with a stick, shouting and cursing. He managed to turn and scramble away just in time to avoid the blows as the stick hit the ground at his heels. Gestas, of course, was out of sight already.

After a time searching around the usual hiding places, Dismas found him hunkered down, feasting on the stolen bread. He looked up at Dismas and grinned.

'I saved you some.' And he handed over the last corner of crust. 'And did you see the look on that man's face when I pushed him? That was so funny. He deserved that.'

Dismas was angry but could not say anything. He took the crust, barely a mouthful.

'You're too slow. I'm not going to save you if you get caught. You're useless. I really don't know why I let you follow me around.'

Despite this sort of regular treatment, Dismas would always follow Gestas' lead. Wherever he wanted to go to scout out, Dismas would trot along behind like a kid following a goat. He never grew tall and strong, even when others did; he was destined to be a short man. But Dismas was more astute and a little cleverer, which Gestas recognised and took advantage of.

Together they had a complementary set of skills for survival on the streets. Dismas knew the relationship was superficial and unfounded. There was no genuine care for each other, but then Gestas had never promised or pretended any such thing. For Dismas, he gleaned a sense of brotherhood when he was with Gestas. Deep down he needed relationship and this was as good a substitute as any. In fact he had no other option. Partnership with Gestas soon became a part of the pattern of his life in the city.

Dismas had a useful skill of protecting them from the Roman patrols. The Romans were ruthless in their control of the city. They would enforce the laws indiscriminately, without any care or compassion, in their mission to maintain the rule of law. Instinctively, the boys knew to avoid any close contact, even to evade being spotted at a distance by the Romans. When scurrying around the city he would put his hand on Gestas' shoulder to indicate for to him to stop. His heightened sense of hearing had been triggered.

'Romans?' Gestas would ask, followed by a few moments of quiet as they listened.

They would then hear the distant clanking of weapons and armour. Usually Dismas could tell how many there were, whether they were two or four abreast, normal pace or double time, and even their likely route, to give them an idea of which direction to escape in. He learned the soldier's regular patrol routes and knew where they were likely to be. If they were to be captured by a patrol, at best they would be beaten or hauled away. At worst, they could meet their end at the hands of the soldiers, right there in the street.

'Six,' Dismas might say. 'In the street up ahead. Heading this way.'

They would dart into the shadows until the patrol had passed and it was safe to carry on. Dismas was clever and this saved them many times.

'They are going to get us one time,' warned Dismas.

'Not before I get them,' bragged Gestas. 'They killed my parents, but not before my father had stuck his dagger into three of them. He was the strongest man ever, and the best fighter! It took five of them to hold him down before they killed him. I am going to kill as many Romans as I can.'

The Roman presence would ebb and flow depending on the tide of rebellion in Jerusalem. At times, when the city was busy, there was a greater presence of soldiers patrolling the streets. An air of restlessness would lead occasionally to riots, bringing a ruthless clamp-down by the Romans. The streets would clear quickly at the end of the day, as a curfew was enforced. At these times there were very few signs of life during the night, leaving the scavengers to complete their job of clearing away the day's mess. These were times that Dismas knew to make himself scarce and keep out of sight.

Most of their time was spent stealing. To start with this was simply to survive, but as they got older, the motivation was increasingly to seek revenge on the people of Jerusalem.

Food was the traditional and more useful bounty, but coins became increasingly attractive. When they got coins there was little they could do with them. The market traders would not allow any of them to stand at their stall to buy anything legitimately. The traders had to keep up appearances, otherwise their normal customers would take their trade elsewhere. They could not risk getting the reputation of doing business with the homeless. But stealing coins did give Dismas pleasure in knowing that he was getting vengeance on the wealthy. And for just a few things, a coin was useful currency.

His hair was usually matted with dust, falling in clumps to his shoulders. When his hair got too heavy and congealed, handfuls would fall out. His scalp was constantly itchy, infested with fleas and lice. One of the older boys who had a knife would cut their hair shorter in exchange for a coin. A hair cut was simply the boy grabbing a handful of hair and sawing the knife through the clumps and knots, as close to the scalp as possible, leaving an uneven mess with a few odd wisps. For another coin he would use the knife to shave off a beard, but that always seemed too much of a risk for Dismas. He would rather let his beard grow fluffy and patchy.

His appearance had deteriorated over the years. Dismas was now unrecognisable from the child who ran away a few years earlier. His clothes were rags, filthy with the grime from his everyday life. Being unwashed and unclean made the street children even more outcast from a society that was obsessed with being spotless. When the clothes got to the point of being more hole than material, he would steal from washing lines or baskets. Nothing fitted well, but it kept him on the right side of decency.

He once stole the shirt off the back of a dead beggar. He had seen the man slumped in a street, opposite the entrance to an alleyway. He had watched him for a whole day as the good people of the city simply stepped over him, swatting the flies from in front of their faces as they did so. The beggar did not move. Dismas was certain he was dead. The rats were scurrying excitedly in between the wall and the body, crawling under his clothes, gnawing on his flesh. At dusk Dismas ran out from the alleyway, grabbed the beggar's shirt with both hands and whipped it quickly over his head. The dead man's arms lifted and then slumped from the garment, like sacks of flour falling from a cart. Dismas scampered away, new clothes in hand, leaving the dead man lying naked in the street.

He felt no remorse. He was glad to have a new shirt and the dead man had no use of it. In any case, the man had been a worthless beggar.

When Dismas first ran away from home he was wearing a pair of leather sandals. Within a few months of life on the streets they were worn through, but only when the heel strap broke on one of them did he have to cast them off. He was reluctant to lose them. His feet would get sore and cut, but to him these sandals were also a final memory of home comforts. In their broken state they hindered his ability to run and agility was so vital for survival. Since discarding them he had never owned or worn shoes. His feet soon became blackened with thick, hard skin on his soles that even thorns from the street found it difficult to penetrate.

The dry months were easier to endure, as long as the water kept flowing in the aqueducts. When the rains came in the winter months, the city became a different place with particular challenges. It was generally quieter, with less produce coming in from the harvests, so there were fewer opportunities to get food. As food was scarce, the market traders and merchants were more protective of what they did have and so they were more careful to minimise any waste.

There was no shelter from the rain, even when cowering in a narrow alleyway. In a shower, his clothes would be soaked through quickly and cold would set in. The grime would run off him until it got to his legs and feet, which would then be doubly filthy as the streets turned from dust into mud. The hooves and cartwheels would cut up the roads, especially the heavy carts bringing in stone for the building works, feeding the ever-expanding city. The donkeys would be cruelly overladen, trudging through the streets looking like their backs would snap at any moment. Occasionally in the wet they would lose their footing and collapse. With a broken leg or simply not able to stand again under the weight, the animals would be left in the street to die.

The Romans' horses added to the filth, the cavalrymen always watching from their elevated position, ready to call in other soldiers to chase away the street children.

One wet day at dusk, Dismas and Gestas heard a group of three or four other street children scurry past, chattering.

'I heard it was empty now,' one of the boys said, 'and far enough back from the main street for the Romans not to bother it.'

Their ears pricked up; they shared a quick glance then immediately followed. A short distance down the street they turned into an alleyway. A couple of blocks down they came to a small courtyard, with three small workshops set around it. The children they were following pushed at a wooden door in the corner and it twisted open, the bottom hinge broken off.

Dismas and Gestas followed quickly behind, without drawing too much attention from the others. As they entered the dark, abandoned shed, they were hit by a heavy scent. The flagstones, walls and roof beams had been infused with the scent from decades of perfumes and oils, worked into the stone and wood, now gently reminding the world of a lifetime of labour in the workshop. It was as if this shelter had been prepared for burial.

'A perfume-maker used to work here,' said a child. 'Last week the Romans dragged him, his wife and his daughter out of here. No idea what they were accused of. They'll never be back.'

'Good,' muttered Gestas. 'It means we can have somewhere to stay dry.'

Inside, the workshop had been wrecked and plundered. Workbenches had been overturned and broken. On the hardened mud floor were shattered pots and vases, smashed for fun by the new residents. Some of the stones from the wall to the workshop next-door were being pulled down, left in a mound of rubble and dust. It was dry and safe, well away from any Roman patrols, and as long as they were quiet then no one would know. As the evening went on, more and more children came in, until every inch of floorspace was occupied.

There was chattering and laughing, as they enjoyed a little relief from the damp, cold night. The chatter soon turned to them telling stories of their antics, the older ones bragging about what they had been able to get away with, telling taller and taller tales. They soon began to speculate about the more gory aspects of life on the streets.

There were many myths circulating amongst the street children about what happened when caught by the Romans. Some said they were taken to Gehenna, their throats cut and left to die on a pile of burning rubbish. Others that they were crucified, or taken to the slave markets and the soldiers pocketed the money. They would never know how much was true or what was made up, but they knew that they dared not take the risk in finding out. Over the years, too many of them had been captured and never seen again.

Dismas slept lightly for a short while, but the chattering and snoring of the other children disturbed him, and the unaccustomed warmth caused him to dream. Riha was with him again. They were running away, being chased. He woke sweating and upset, met by the heavy scent of the rare oils and perfumes hanging around in the darkness.

There was some giggling and laughing in the far corner.

'There's a dog in here.'

'The mangey thing has crawled in.'

One child picked up a piece of wood and was poking at it, as it shivered with fear, pinned in the corner.

'Let's kill it. Clear at least one other vermin from our patch,' and there were mutterings of approval.

'Stone it! Stone it!' a chant went up.

The children picked up stones from where the wall was pulled down and began to hurl them at the dog.

Dismas could not witness this. It was all so wrong. He had to escape. He darted out of the door to the sound of pathetic yelps and howls from the poor creature. It was just the same as them really, simply trying to survive.

The chanting subsided as he stole away from the deserted workshop, returning to the streets. There was no easy way to escape his situation.

The dark and wet winter nights were especially miserable. At nightfall Dismas usually took to seeking solitude. It was safer. He also needed time away from Gestas, whose continuous complaining and whining would penetrate even his blank exterior. In these lonely times, he would think again that he may have been better off back at his aunt's and uncle's house. *It can't be any worse than where I am now? If I can survive here then surely I could have survived back there?* But he knew deep down it was never going to happen. There was no way he could face the shame and hatred that would be directed at him from his uncle and aunt. They hated him. They did not want him back. At least here he could be on his own.

On his wanderings through the city streets he occasionally found himself at the end of the row of houses where his uncle and aunt had lived. He would pause in the shadows and watch the house. He never had any intention of speaking to them. He was just curious. *Were they still living there? Were they still alive? If they saw me, would they even care that I was still alive?* But at the first sign of any movement from within the house or the neighbours' houses, he would quickly disappear, convincing himself that they still did not want him in their lives.

Lurking around some nearby food stalls one grey morning, Dismas did see the familiar figure of his aunt, standing in a queue, waiting to be served at a bread stall. He could only see the side of her face, but it was definitely her. His heart raced, both fearful and excited that she may catch him. She looked old and tired. He stood by a wall at the edge of the street, a little closer than he would normally be, half hoping she would spot him. She took and paid for her bread, then turned in his direction. Life froze for a moment. She caught his eye and paused, briefly looking directly at him. His heart was pounding so hard as he dared to allow a glimmer of hope to nudge its way in. His mind raced. *Maybe uncle has died? Maybe she would want me back? Perhaps she would drop her bread, embrace me and sweep me off back home to warmth, shelter and food, celebrating me being found?*

It was just a fleeting glimpse from her, before she turned away, to walk hurriedly back down the road, grumbling to herself.

'Those children are disgusting,' she mumbled, with a look of repulsion on her face.

She could not recognise any part of him. That small, shy, clean little boy whom she had known, had long since disappeared. This wiry street urchin with long matted hair, patches of pathetic fluffy beard on his face, blackened bare feet and in filthy rags, did not trigger any recognition from her at all.

Dismas was shattered. His heart was emptied. He could not cry or scream or shout or lash out. He had no one to talk to and, even if he did, he would not be able to express the pain he was now suffering. Inside, his mind was spiralling out of control. *They never loved me. They never wanted me. I killed my mother. I am a murderer and I deserve to be on the streets. They are not my real family anyway. I am better off where I am now. If I was still there my uncle would have killed me by now.*

Anger and rage became his closest companions, haunting and tormenting every moment of his life, whether awake or asleep.

Chapter 8
Captured

I, the LORD, have called you in righteousness; I will take hold of your hand. I will keep you and will make you to be a covenant for the people and a light for the Gentiles, to open eyes that are blind, to free captives from prison and to release from the dungeon those who sit in darkness. (Isaiah 42:6-7)

He was now dedicated to stealing and scavenging, to seek maximum revenge, fuelled by hatred. Even thieving from those who themselves would need to beg to survive. Beggars normally had some sort of disability like blindness or leprosy. Dismas had little about him that would generate any sympathy from passers-by. He was simply a scrawny street boy. No one could see his story. There was nothing unusual about him.

In a quiet moment on the street, he once came alongside a blind beggar who used to ply his trade near to the Essene Gate, at the southern end of the city. The man was sitting on the ground, leaning against the whitewashed wall of a house, within sight of the gates. Dismas had intended to sneak up on him to steal the bowl of coins, but as he approached, the beggar sensed he was there and spoke to him.

'Can you spare a coin?'

Dismas did not reply. The beggar instinctively placed his hands on the rim of the bowl that was on the ground in front of him. The man could smell that this was someone who lived on the streets.

'If you are a thief then get away. You are not having this.'

Dismas did not want to wrestle him for the coins, but just stood there staring at him, unsure how to react.

'You can come and help if you want to?' the beggar sensed in Dismas his hesitancy to steal. 'We may do better working together?'

Dismas was unsure if the beggar had taken pity on him, or whether it was convenient for him too. But he quietly sat down in the dirt next to him. He stared at the beggar's closed eyes, safe in the knowledge that he would not be seen and the old man would not be offended. The man's small eyeballs were sunk deep into his skull, hidden behind thin and veiny eyelids. He turned his face towards Dismas, offered a toothless grin and opened his eyelids to reveal eyeballs devoid of colour. The pink bloodshot eyeballs surrounded white irises, with no black pupil in the centre. They were white and weeping.

Dismas turned away quickly, not for fear of eye contact, but because the sight disgusted him. He edged away from the man to avoid being too close. He did not want to catch whatever disease this man had.

The two of them together did trigger more sympathy from passersby, who must have assumed they were father and son. They began to generate a healthy haul of coins.

'You don't say much, do you?' the beggar said after a while. 'Can you talk? What's your name?'

'Dismas,' he mumbled.

'What a great name! That's a lovely name. You should be proud of that name. I have not seen a sunset for over twenty years. When I could see I used to love watching the sun set in the evening. That brings back such lovely memories for me. Sunset. What a special name you have.'

With every word, anger and rage was building up inside Dismas, consuming him until it had to burst out. He had to get away. He leaped to his feet, grabbed the pot of coins from in front of them and ran away without looking back. He had stolen the blind beggar's takings for the day.

Dismas retreated to the shadows for a few days. He knew that what he had done was wrong and unfair. *Why did I panic like that? Why did those feeling make me just want to flee?* The thoughts chased around inside his head and just made him dislike himself even more. The guilt and sorrow were eating away at him. He decided to try to make it right.

A week after running away from the beggar, Dismas returned to that same part of the city, with half an idea to say he was sorry. He wanted to, but was not certain he would be able to. When he saw the same beggar again in the same spot, he approached but hesitated. As usual he found that he had no idea what to say. In his confusion, he simply sat down next to the man as though nothing had changed between them.

'It's you, isn't it? I know it's you. Why did you do that to me before? I thought we were helping each other. I would have shared with you.'

Again, Dismas had no words to answer or explain why he had behaved like he had. He could only sit there in silence.

'Answer me!' and his shouts became increasingly frustrated at the lack of response.

Inside, Dismas was so confused. He had been feeling some guilt and wanted to be able to apologise, but his mind was so fogged. He could find no way to express anything. Panic was rising.

The blind beggar began to shout more, cursing Dismas at the top of his voice. A tirade of abuse bringing unwanted attention from those in the street around them.

Dismas instinctively reacted, jumped up and ran into the shadows nearby, leaving the beggar ranting furiously. He wanted the boy arrested.

He wanted justice. He continued to scream and shout, very soon drawing the attention of the Roman guards near the gate.

Dismas watched on as they arrived at the scene with no intention of listening to his story. They simply beat the man into silence. When he was quiet, they dragged his limp, bloodied body outside the gate and dumped him on the side of the road. Dismas edged towards the gate and peered out. He could see the man bleeding, breathing heavily and moaning. His response was to slip away quickly, leaving the blind man to his end.

He wanted not to care. He even tried to convince himself that he had done the city a favour, helping to get another beggar cleared off the streets. The city had one less mouth to feed, so there was more opportunity for himself.

He never saw that blind beggar again.

Death was no stranger to anyone who lived on the streets. Life was fragile and the threat of death lurked around, waiting to pounce unexpectedly.

'Look what I've got,' bragged Gestas one morning. He took out a knife from under his cloak. It had a short rusty blade, sharpened on both edges, with a chipped wooden handle.

'You know that tall kid who always hangs around the Hippodrome, with the beard. I saw him drop it in the gutter as he ran across the road. He never came back for it, so I took it.'

Dismas was nervous. Not only did this raise the stakes for them, but he knew that Gestas in possession of a knife was a dangerous prospect.

'I need a knife,' and he held it up in front of his face, inspecting it. 'Now all the others will have to respect me.'

Later on that day the two of them were scouting out a fruit stall that was packing up for the day. As the trader left, he discarded a few bruised peaches in the gutter. Just as they were about to pick them up, another child raced out in front of them, grabbed the fruit and ran.

'Come here! That was ours!' shouted Gestas, incensed. 'Come on, let's get her!' Dismas followed on as Gestas sprinted after her, out of sight.

Dismas caught up with Gestas a few streets away, walking back towards him. In his hand was the fruit. He had clearly caught up with the girl. Dismas glanced at his other hand, which was gripping the bloodied knife. Gestas had used it.

'She won't do that again!' Gestas sounded triumphant. 'Here, have a peach.' And he tossed a peach towards Dismas who caught it but could only stare at it.

Gestas grinned and slurped as the peach juice dribbled down his chin. 'What? Not going to eat yours?'

'No,' answered Dismas. He had no appetite for it. He was sickened at what he had been dragged into. Gestas grabbed it from him.

'I'll have it then. I earned it anyway. You did nothing. I wonder why I even bother trying to help you out. There's no point you being here.'

Dismas sloped off to be on his own, with faint echoes of distant memories creeping back into his head. Ones that he did not want to revisit.

It was a few days before he could face being alongside Gestas again. When he did, things were different. Gestas was the same; still arrogant and ignorant. But Dismas was growing so weary of it all. The deceit, mistrust, death and hatred were grinding him down. He found it difficult to care any more about anything they were doing. He tagged along, but his heart was not in it. Deep down, he knew that what they were doing was not right.

The monotony of life continued but with more risk now. News had spread quickly that Gestas was armed, which had increased his status on the streets. It meant that other boys were more inclined to hang around him, knowing it was better for them to be his ally than his enemy.

Dismas spent more time away from him when he could, but despite the direction that Gestas was heading, there was still the draw that they were a good partnership to work the crowds. The richest pickings for coins was always around the temple and the chaotic temple courts, where moneychangers, lenders and merchants would gather. Especially around festival times – and the people of Jerusalem seemed to have a lot of festivals.

The crowds would be larger, swollen with visitors from outside the city. These strangers did not seem to know the dangers posed by the likes of Dismas and Gestas. Grabbing money bags from their belts seemed so easy in a pressing crowd.

Festival time brought a greater presence of temple guards, so they needed to take some care. But the street children also knew they had a role to play in this game. Outside the temple gates, as pilgrims would enter the Court of the Gentiles, these religious visitors would need to be seen to be doing the right thing, giving to the poor. They would mutter about the importance of caring for the widows and orphans. It was the only safe place for the street children to be out in the daylight, the only time in the city when they were actually needed. Dismas was happy to provide this service to the pilgrims, happy to take their coins or morsels of food to ease their consciences, even if they performed this act of worship without offering a smile or eye contact.

The visitors to Jerusalem were generally in awe of the city and especially the temple, believing that God himself lived there. Dismas simply thought this made them seem even more stupid. *How could God live so close to all this poverty, filth and depravation? If only the pilgrims knew what my life is like, then surely they would know that God could not be so close?*

Crowds would surge to the temple, through the outer gates into the expanse of courtyard, where animals, children and women were still allowed. The street children could get in there but never any further. The crowds talked of God being inside and how he needed their sacrifices. *I know they will never let me in there to meet him.*

It was one busy Passover festival that led to his demise. This particular year, Dismas could sense an excitement in the crowds and a nervousness from the temple guards. They were on edge, more vigilant than normal. The mood was volatile and the crowds were larger. The temple guards had been doubled and an extra legion of Roman soldiers was patrolling the city. The rumours of rebellion and insurgence were strong and Dismas was wary. Chaos was not far away, the mood of the crowd swaying between celebration and anarchy, with seemingly very little needed to trigger it.

Inside the temple courts, Dismas and Gestas were doing their best to perform their duties, a fine balance between keeping a low profile and being available to the pilgrims, without attracting too much attention from the guards.

From the middle of the courts there was suddenly an uproar. Shouts, screams and the sound of crashing tables. Some people fled away from the source of the noise, others rushed towards it, confusion and shrieks in many different languages.

'Let's take a look,' said Gestas and the two of them quickly weaved through the crowd to see what was going on.

In the middle of the courts they saw a mess of overturned tables. The moneychangers were desperately trying to gather their coins that had been scattered across the cobblestones, while pilgrims were grabbing at the ground, unable to subdue their own greed. Some of the stalls that had been selling animals for sacrifice had been thrown over, leaving doves flapping up from their smashed cages, with a trail of feathers in the air behind them. The goats and sheep were panicking, their bleats adding to the general mayhem that ensued.

On the far side of the courts, they saw a group of pilgrims surrounded by children. A man at the centre of the crowd was roaring as he grabbed the edge of another table and hurled it over, sending coins into the air around them. Stallholders were shouting, temple guards were racing towards them. The group made a hasty exit through the gates in the corner of the courts.

Whatever this was about did not concern the two boys, but they were determined to benefit from it. Their instinct was to dive to the ground and grab as many of the coins as they could.

From all corners of the temple, the guards came running, bellowing at the crowds. The two boys had just a few seconds to snatch as much as they could.

'We have to go now,' shouted Dismas, tugging at Gestas. They leaped to their feet and raced for the nearest way out with their fists tightly holding on to their stolen coins. They were spotted and closely followed by two temple guards, shouting at them to stop.

They escaped the temple courts through the outer gate, leaped down the steps and raced along the busy street, desperately trying not to drop any of their spoils. In their wake there was a lot of shouting from the bewildered crowds and the two guards were still in pursuit. Dismas thought they should have jumped into the safety of a dark alleyway, but Gestas just kept running down the street, and so as usual he stayed quiet and followed.

At the end of the street they turned the corner and at full pace came face to face with a patrol of Roman soldiers who were quick-marching towards the temple. There was no way to escape.

'Grab them,' screamed one of soldiers, and they instinctively seized the boys by the arms, causing them to spill their handfuls of coins onto the road. The temple guards arrived a few seconds behind, breathing heavily and pleased with their good fortune.

'We saw these two steal from the temple,' reported one.

'They were with that group of troublemakers that are hanging around. The ones we have been warned about. They were all in the temple and threw over the tables. Most of them escaped, but we saw these two run off with the coins.'

'They are rebels then,' announced a Roman soldier, passing full and final judgment.

'That's a lie!' screamed Gestas, who broke one arm free from the soldiers' grasp. They all saw Gestas reach into his tunic and Dismas knew he was going for his knife.

'Blade!' the soldier shouted, to warn the others, and he drew his sword. With one skilled blow, to the sound of metal on metal, the knife was knocked out of Gestas' hand. He let out a shriek and fell to the ground, clutching his wrist.

Two soldiers picked him up by his arms. Gestas just could not help himself, still struggling, trying to wriggle free of the soldiers' grip. But the more he fought them the tighter they held him. One of the soldiers got fed up and struck him with the back of his hand, the studded leather wrist guard slicing open a gash on his cheek. Gestas whimpered like a dog and submitted.

By contrast, Dismas did not struggle at all. He had very little fight left in him. He was resigned to his destiny, obeying every command from the soldiers, allowing them to bind his hands and lead him away. Inside he was consumed with fear. He knew all the stories of what happened when street children were captured. Romans were vicious and unforgiving.

The soldiers spent a short time talking to the temple guards. There was a lot of nodding and agreement before the two guards collected the coins from the ground and departed.

'Take these insurgents away!' ordered the commander. 'They are guilty of stealing.'

The two of them were taken off by four of the soldiers in the direction of one of the city jails. There would be no justice or trial for the likes of them.

For Dismas and Gestas, their error of judgment was to be their death sentence.

Chapter 9
Reconnection

Therefore, there is now no condemnation for those who are in Christ Jesus, because through Christ Jesus the law of the Spirit of life set me free from the law of sin and death. (Romans 8:1-2)

Habib was not used to holding on to his memories. As Dismas, he had always lived his life in the present. Just existing from day to day was all that he had been able to cope with. He had always assumed it was normal to have a memory as poor as his, but the truth was that remembering was never a luxury he felt able to allow himself. Memories were nearly all hurtful or shameful. The details of his life had only ever brought him torment and self-loathing. They did not deserve to be recalled. The few happy memories he had did not offer any comfort. They simply brought on emotions of loss and grief.

Reclining on this blue stone, going back over his story now with Jesus, was a brand-new experience, surprisingly easy and cathartic for him. The previous dullness that had accompanied his existence, the self-protecting suppression of all emotions and feelings that had been necessary for his very survival on the streets, was now subsiding.

Looking into the eyes of Jesus, Habib felt no condemnation or shame. He felt released. Jesus looked back at him with pure compassion. As Habib's story was being recounted, every hurt and pain that Jesus heard brought a tear to his eyes. Jesus had felt it all. Whilst relating all of this to Jesus, Habib felt that his emotions were lining up, being restored and rebuilt. The process was bringing him healing as his mind was starting to understand it all. It led him to one obvious question that he had to voice.

'Where was God in all of this?'

Jesus could see it was an honest question. In his past life it may have been driven by anger and a perceived sense of injustice. Now it was a genuine and fair question. Whatever the motivation, at this point in his rehabilitation, Jesus knew it was the right one for him to know the answer to.

'Father accepted you into his kingdom at the moment you were born, when you were orphaned.' His eyes looked deeply into Habib's. His words spoke directly into Habib's soul. 'God loves you and watched over you through every moment of your life. He had a plan for you and his plan led you to be here.'

'Why did it have to be so tough though?' There was no accusation in his voice. He was pondering.

'Every one of Father's creations is given the opportunity to choose for themselves. Like everyone else, you made choices, as did the people around you and those who were responsible for you,' replied Jesus. 'Some of the actions that other people chose did not work out well for your story. They brought you pain and suffering. But a loving Father has to allow all his children to make their own choices in complete freedom. If they were not allowed this freedom, how could his children choose to love him back? No one can be forced to love another. They have to do it willingly, otherwise it is not love.'

'I see,' said Habib. There was a pause in the conversation as he thought this through. It was so new to him, but he did understand. 'I did so many wrong things. I don't see why I am here.' He did not really mean anyone else to hear these words.

'We still loved you when you did those things. No person has ever lived a perfect life free from mistakes. However much we do not like your sin, we don't condemn you for it. We never abandon you. In fact, the only way we could rescue you was for me to take everyone's punishment for all their sin, on the cross. I chose to do that so that you could be saved.'

Habib rocked backwards, as though he had been pushed in the chest. He looked at Jesus wide-eyed as this revelation struck him. Jesus had chosen to take the punishment so that he could be free. Doubts flashed through his mind. *Surely I am not worthy to be saved like this?*

As he stared at Jesus his doubts melted away. His feelings were changing. He could only be in complete awe of him. He began to realise how thankful he was for what Jesus had completed.

Habib recognised that nothing from his story had shocked or surprised Jesus. He now knew that it was all already known. He was finding it hard to believe, after all he had been through, that someone else had taken any of his punishment. He had always felt that he had been dealt his own fair share.

'I have been telling you my story, but this is not new to you, is it? You knew it all already. Why did you need me to go through the pain of telling you all this?' Habib sounded a little more indignant than he had intended.

'Telling us your story has not been for me. This has been for you. Every person spends time recounting their story to us when they first arrive in heaven. We listen and give everyone as much time as they need to be able to fully understand it. In doing this, you have been able to confess all that has gone before and you can now see the Father's hand on your life. It leads you to a place of forgiveness.'

Jesus explained further. 'You know that your actions and words caused damage and pain to others. You lived in a broken and hurting world. All that pain caused by you to others was a result of poor choices. And you have now been forgiven. Completely.'

Jesus leaned forward, took Habib's hand in his and looked at him directly in the eyes.

'You need to know that we forgive you. Forgiveness is a part of the healing process. I have fully forgiven you and you are accepted into heaven.'

'Thank you,' responded Habib, genuinely accepting this life-saving gift of forgiveness, without fully realising how important it was.

After a pause for this revelation to take root, Jesus continued.

'There is another step for you to take. You cannot hold on to the bitter root that is unforgiveness. You have to let it go. Like those bitter mustard plants you had to chew on, even the smallest of seeds will grow to be a large plant. You have confessed your story to me, you are forgiven, so now you must also forgive.'

Habib was taken aback by this. He had never felt the need to forgive. *Why do I need to forgive anyone?* The blank look on Habib's face told Jesus that he still did not understand.

'Every person has the freedom to make choices,' Jesus continued. 'Choices to do the right thing or not. If they want to, everyone can choose to love. In love, you can put your own pains to one side. In fact, I know that someone can carry all manner of pains out of love for others. This is what sacrifice is.

'So, when you make the choice to love rather than hate, you discover that you are able to speak out forgiveness. Habib, in your life, you suffered a lot of hurt and anguish at the hands of other people. If you can forgive them, then you will be freed. When we know that we are forgiven, then we can live in love and discover that we can forgive others. And you need to know that you have been completely forgiven.'

These concepts were taking time for Habib to fully understand.

'I have an idea. Let me introduce you to someone.'

Jesus released Habib's hand and stood up. Habib stayed reclining on the large blue stone while he watched Jesus walk to the edge of the clearing. When he got there he paused, looked back and smiled reassuringly at Habib. Jesus reached his arm into the trees so that it was out of Habib's sight. As he pulled it back into view, Jesus was holding someone else's hand. He walked back towards the stone, leading a man by the hand.

Habib was wondering to himself who this man may be. *Perhaps someone to explain things a bit more simply to me.* But as they got closer, Habib jumped up in surprise. He realised that Jesus was walking towards him, hand in hand with his uncle.

The first thought that flashed across his mind was *Why is my uncle here at all?* It made no sense to him. He never expected to see him again. He thought he should feel frightened or angry, but none of these feelings came. To his surprise he felt no panic or fear. He felt no hatred. He just felt an all-surpassing calmness emanating from the presence of Jesus. He trusted him.

His uncle was smiling. Habib did not remember ever having seen his uncle smile before and it disarmed him. As his uncle came close, he held out both his hands. His dead arm was healed. Habib held out his hands too, to greet the man, and they grasped each other firmly by the wrists, as two men with a tight bond between them. As they gripped each other, there was a flow of light from each man that spiralled down their arms, wrapping around their wrists, intertwining and bonding them together.

As they gazed directly into each other's eyes, a powerful cold wind blew across them, awakening Habib to things he had not seen or known before. At the moment of contact, there was an instant understanding in Habib's heart. He was able to see the whole story unfold in his mind.

He saw his uncle's compassion for him.

He saw how distressed his uncle had been on that day when his youngest brother's wife had died, giving birth to her firstborn son. It was meant to be such a joyous occasion, but it was destroyed by death. His uncle saw how his precious little brother was consumed with a violent fury, his future torn away, his dreams shattered, overwhelmed with grief.

He saw his uncle's desperate desire to rescue the infant from the raging hands of his broken father and the certain death that would have followed if the child had remained there another moment.

He saw the grief that took hold of the family and tore apart the bond between the two brothers. The bitterness and anger that ate away at every part of their lives, eventually driving apart their brotherhood.

He saw his uncle's kindness in taking Habib in, giving him a home. His intentions and motives were so true and selfless. But it went sour. Money and food were scarce. All his own children had left the home and income was limited. Life was difficult and the child was a strain. He would often go hungry himself so the child could eat, causing him to be resentful and angry.

He saw how tormented his uncle became when his arm had been crushed. The constant pain. That falling stone destroyed more than just flesh and blood. It destroyed a livelihood. He was an older man and work was impossible to find. As he lost control of his life, he lost control of his emotions. His temper became shorter and uncontrollable. But Habib could see his uncle's deep sorrow for those moments when the anger had driven him to lash out at the young child.

He saw how, from the moment that Habib ran away from home, his uncle had roamed the streets of Jerusalem for many days and nights, desperately searching, asking everyone he met, shouting his name through the city.

He saw his uncle's brokenness, utterly distraught at having failed his nephew and his brother. The child was gone, probably dead by now. He lost hope, knowing how impossible it would be for a precious young child to survive alone on the streets of Jerusalem.

He saw his uncle gripped by guilt and pain for his remaining years, crying out to God on his deathbed for forgiveness and for Habib to be rescued. Habib could hear the echo of these heartfelt prayers of a dying man, prayers that had been answered.

He now saw the full measure of the forgiveness of God. He now understood that forgiveness was also his gift to give.

Habib saw it all. He had wrongly judged his uncle. That was not his role. Judgment was a responsibility that he should not bear. It had been tearing him apart. All that he needed to do was forgive.

The wind subsided and the two men looked deeply into each other's eyes and exchanged a lasting smile. No more words were needed. They both understood. They remained there for some time whilst Habib was getting used to this very different perception of his uncle.

'I am quite surprised to see you here!' Habib eventually said and the two men laughed.

'You will be surprised who is here, rather than who is not,' Jesus said and smiled warmly at them. 'Now, let's do this.'

Jesus motioned to them both to sit down on the plinth, facing each other. He then placed between them a silver plate and a wooden cup. This cup, a chalice, was carved to look like a tree, with roots as its base, the stem intricately carved to look like a tree trunk, flowing up to create a network of branches with leaves and fruits decorating it. The silver plate had words engraved around its edges, in a beautiful flowing script. In the centre of the plate was some bread.

'This is manna,' said Jesus. 'Heaven's sustenance. Taste a little.'

Habib cautiously took the bread and tore off a piece. He hesitated as he put it to his lips. He could not eat. Something in his soul stopped him. He could hear in his mind the calls that the lepers used to cry out as they walked towards the city gates, 'Unclean, unclean!' He did not feel worthy enough to eat.

'I can't do this.'

'If you speak out forgiveness, you can eat,' said Jesus.

Habib had seen the power of forgiveness on his uncle's life and realised now that the same was needed for himself. But he had no idea how to forgive. What could he possibly say that would be able to forgive so many people who had wronged him, through his whole life?

'What do I say?' whispered Habib.

'Just say the words from your heart. The words you choose will release it all to me.'

Habib looked towards Jesus nervously, unsure what was going to happen next. His mind was blank. Then he remembered the words he had heard Jesus himself say, not so long ago. He muttered towards the ground, hoping no one would hear. 'Father God, I forgive them, for they did not know what they were doing.'

Jesus grinned.

'That was so perfect!'

Habib looked up and grinned back. He put the bread to his lips and ate. He closed his eyes as the manna went into his mouth and he could see the faces of so many people flashing through his mind. People who had hurt him, insulted him and wounded him. People he loved who had deserted him. People who had abandoned him and caused so much distress. He knew these were all the people he now needed to forgive. He could not carry the burden of judging them. As Jesus said, he needed to release them. To let the unforgiveness go. As he did so, he felt freed.

His uncle and Jesus also ate some of the manna, the three of them sharing the blessing of forgiveness.

'There is more,' said Jesus, as he lifted the wooden chalice and handed it to Habib. 'This is heaven's wine. For your complete healing.'

Habib had never tasted wine before. It was reserved for the wealthy or the important, not for a child from the streets like him. He was quite excited to try it. He reached out and took the cup in both hands, held it to his lips and sipped. It was more than he could have ever imagined.

The liquid invigorated his mouth, awakened to the multitude of new flavours. He could feel it trickle down his throat and a warmth spread through his body and limbs. As he looked in front of him, at his hands holding the cup, the scars on his wrists began to tingle. He watched as the scars began to dissolve until they had completely disappeared. His skin was pure and clear, as though the scars had never existed.

Wide-eyed, he glanced down at his feet. The same was happening to those scars too. They were gone, leaving only smooth, clean, perfect skin.

He felt his legs twitch and flex a little, as though an energy was passing through them. The muscles were contracting, tightening the ligaments, pulling the bones into line.

'You are healed,' said Jesus. 'My body was broken and my blood was shed so that you can be whole.'

In his excitement, Habib quickly passed the cup to his uncle in case he dropped it. He looked back to his hands in amazement, then lifted them up in front of himself, like a young child showing his parents something special. He could not help himself from shouting excitedly, 'Look, my scars have gone!'

He jumped to his feet and took a few steps around the stone. 'And my legs are healed. I don't limp!'

'You have a new body,' said Jesus.

With a broad smile across his face, Habib jumped and skipped around the clearing. The child in him was released to celebrate unhindered. He was liberated. Physically healed and more complete than ever.

He became entirely lost in the new-found freedom that had overtaken him. He was dancing, spinning and skipping around the stones, across the clearing, jumping over the stream, overtaken with delight. Each movement was a release, an act of thanks and worship in response to his healing.

He did not know how long he was in this state of ecstasy. For the first time he was simply able to enjoy being alive. When he eventually stopped bounding around, he found he was alone again. Jesus and his uncle had departed, but he did not mind. He was perfectly content. He knew there would be more and he would see them again.

He lay down on the grass next to the blue plinth, comfortably basking in the warming light. He was happy in his own thoughts, amazed at the course of events that had brought him to this place.

Chapter 10
Condemned by the Law

For all have sinned and fall short of the glory of God, and are justified freely by his grace through the redemption that came by Christ Jesus. (Romans 3:23-24)

Habib stayed in the woodland clearing for some time, resting alone on the grass beside the stone plinth. He felt so peaceful there. The sound of the trees comforted him, accompanied by the sounds from the gently flowing water in the nearby stream. He had no need for anything more. That drive within him to seek out safety, that had been consuming and directing every moment of his previous life, was now gone. He was safe.

His body felt whole and there was a new clarity to his thoughts, with a revelatory understanding of why he had become the character that he was. All bitterness and blame had left him. Purity was becoming a new best friend.

As he pondered what had just happened, he realised that telling his story to Jesus had released him. It was clearing his head. There was more though. The story did not end there.

His mind turned to the course of events that had led him to be in heaven. It was important that he recounted his last few days of being Dismas and he knew he was now ready to face it.

*

When he and Gestas were captured on the street by that Roman patrol, they were rapidly marched away from the scene, Gestas with blood oozing from the wound on his cheek.

'Get them out of here quickly,' one of the soldiers ordered. 'We don't want their co-conspirators attempting any sort of rescue.'

They were taken directly to the nearest jail, adjacent to the Praetorium, Herod's palace. They were dragged through the gates into a dusty courtyard. The soldiers holding them reported to the prison guards.

'These are two of the rebels. Caught stealing money from the temple. Part of the uprising.'

They were directed to the nearest building. A guard slid across the bolt on the outside and the two thieves were pushed violently into the cell. The iron door slammed behind them.

There was no trial or justice system for a street wretch. Dismas had been caught in the act of thieving and the testimony of the temple guards was all that was needed to prove him a criminal. Not just a thief, but apparently an insurgent too.

He was resigned to his fate from the moment of his arrest. Capture and crucifixion at the hands of the Romans had been a driving fear ever since his beard had begun to grow, an outward sign to the authorities that he would then be old enough to be executed. He had often witnessed these punishments play out in the city and knew that his own body would now end up being savaged by dogs and vultures, like those he had seen from the city walls. Deserted and forsaken in this cell, guilty, destined for the slave's punishment of crucifixion, his life was worthless and expendable. He even thought it was deserved. Being a prisoner did not feel much different to him. He had never known much freedom, having been a slave to his circumstances for his entire life.

Dismas was fully compliant, entirely consumed by his own thoughts. He no longer had any appetite for life and could see no point to his existence. No one would be making representations to the Romans to plead for his release. He had just a few hours or days left.

Inside the jail the smell of decay and filth was even worse than the streets, with no breeze to relieve them from the heat and the stench. There were eight or ten other dirty and angry men with them in the small cell, and no safe shadows for Dismas to hide away in. The streets had been safer. There was little conversation, just the occasional groan and whimper. Dismas slumped down in the dirt. The man next to him tutted.

'Rebels, eh?' he muttered. 'You won't be here long. They won't want you stirring up any uprising in here.'

Dismas just stared at the ground, fearful to meet his eyes. He dared not ask him why he was in the prison, but could not help noticing a piece missing from his right ear and some letters recently branded on his upper arm, sure signs of being an escaped slave.

Gestas was even more unbearable than usual. He could not cope with being in the cell, moaning about the smell, the heat, the thirst and the pain from his injuries. His complaining and groaning seemed endless, despite regular punches and kicks from other inmates, in their attempt to quieten him down.

That first day passed, followed by a night of terror. Even if he would have been able to, Dismas dared not sleep. In the corner of the cell he shrunk back as far into the darkness as he could, as if he were trying to be swallowed up by the walls.

On the second day of their imprisonment, soon after sunrise, Gestas pushed his way to the front of the cell and lifted his face towards the small opening at the top of the wall. He started to shout at the guards, protesting his innocence.

'I did nothing. I am not a rebel. I had nothing to do with them. I shouldn't be here.'

The prison guards ignored him, but he continued. The longer it went on, the more he lost control, pouring out a deluge of obscenities. The vitriol was a reflection of his lifetime of hatred for a world that had given him nothing. A guard eventually came over to the cell. Of course, they had seen it all and heard it all before. They were not going to waste their energies on punishing Gestas.

'No water or food for this cell today,' one guard shouted into the cell and then walked away.

It took a short while for the reality of this announcement to register with Gestas. As his shouting subsided, it was rapidly replaced by the loud grumblings from the other prisoners. Gestas had his protesting quickly beaten out of him.

Over the next few days there was little change. One or two prisoners arrived to replace those that were dragged off elsewhere. They had no idea when their time may come. With a sentence like that hanging over them the guards did not waste any provisions on them. When they did get some food or water, it was only enough to keep them alive, to ensure they would still be around to suffer the looming punishment.

Dismas was resigned to the fact that it would be over soon and he had yielded to the circumstances. He had no energy or fight left in him. His destiny was inevitable. He even felt a trace of relief that the battle he had been fighting his whole life was now coming to an end.

Life was limited in the cell. The atmosphere was calmer once Gestas had taken his beating, just punctuated with the occasional groan or moan. There was very little chatter, each prisoner lost in the depths of his own thoughts. The heat was unbearable, baking the smells of the men's incarceration.

The other men would claim the prime positions towards the back of the cell, as far from the door as possible, furthest from the guard's view. Dismas assumed his role as the lowest in the cell hierarchy, pushed to the front by the other inmates. He took to squatting in a corner of the front wall, by the door. At least crouched here, there was some relief from the acrid air, as he peered through the grille of the door to observe the comings and goings in the prison courtyard.

In the early hours of the morning of their fourth day in the cell, before dawn, there was a lot of excitement out in the courtyard with a prisoner from one of the other cells. Soldiers and prison guards were busy in all directions, carrying torches that lit the courtyard, making their shadows jump across the walls. A cockerel crowed nearby, stirring life back into the cell. Looking out through the grille, Dismas could see a man being led outside, accompanied by an unusually large group of soldiers. This man did not look especially threatening and he was not struggling. He was a good height with toned muscles, clearly a man who worked a physical job. His hair was of dark curls and he had a short beard, not long like the religious types. He did not look like the usual prisoner to be found in a jail cell.

He was bound at the wrists with his arms in front of him. He stayed calm even whilst he was being pushed around heavy-handedly by the guards. They led him out of the gates and quiet returned to the jail. Dismas thought nothing more of it. An hour later, as first light was appearing, they brought him back through the gates. The courtyard sprung into life again as more guards came out to look at what was happening with this prisoner. The excitement was building, the guards now baying for blood like a pack of barking dogs.

'Pilate has just ordered this one to be flogged,' shouted their commander. Dismas now saw the reason for the excitement. The Romans were cruel and they so enjoyed a flogging.

'Erastus! Prepare yourself. We need you to have some fun with this one.' A loud cheer went up from the whole company.

Catching glimpses through the assembly of prison guards and Roman soldiers, Dismas watched two of them step forward. They grabbed at the man's robe and tore it from him, throwing it into the dust. They were taunting and jeering, enjoying every moment. Another guard produced a soldier's scarlet cape which they hung loosely over his shoulders.

'Now he is a king!' and a cheer went up.

They mocked as they made the prisoner stand in the centre of the courtyard, forcing a staff into his hand.

A chant rose from the crowd: 'This king needs a crown!' Someone had twisted together what looked like twigs, still with the thorns on them, which they pushed on to the top of the prisoner's head. Dismas could see him wince as it was then forced down into his scalp. Blood trickled down his head and neck from where the thorns had pierced his skin.

As this man stood in the courtyard, the crowd of guards surrounding him began to jeer 'Hail, King of the Jews.'

Dismas did not understand. *Why are they taunting him? If this man is a king, why are they treating him like a criminal? What has he done to make them torture him like this?*

The chanting from the crowd of soldiers grew louder as they became increasingly excited. Some of them thought it amusing to kneel in front of him and bow down in mock worship. Others cleared their throat and spat at him. Dismas remembered how that had felt.

One guard grabbed the staff from the prisoner's hand, jumped behind him and struck him with it, hitting him on the side of his body.

'Prophesy then!' he squealed. 'Who was it who hit you?!'

This was met with loud laughter from the guards. The staff was then passed around for others to have a go, the prisoner taking blows to the body and head. His tormentors then tore the scarlet robes from his shoulders and left him standing there, naked. Dismas knew the

Roman's reputation for cruelty, but this was already beyond what he thought possible.

'That's enough now!' ordered the commander in charge. 'Erastus. Your turn.' And another cheer went up.

That is when they flogged him.

The prisoner was pulled towards the scourging post, in the centre of the courtyard. His bound hands were lifted up and over the top of the post, so he could not escape. His hands tightly grasped the post in readiness, knuckles whitening, every muscle in his body tensed.

Dismas had heard about the brutality of this but witnessing it first-hand was beyond anything from the stories. The guard called Erastus stepped forward carrying a whip. He was a tall barrel-chested man, with muscles in his arms that looked as though they could generate a lot of power. His whip was made of a strong wooden stick, about the length of his arm, with six leather straps fixed to one end. Small metal balls and pieces of what looked like sharp bones were stitched into each of the leather straps.

All the other guards stood back in a wide arc, giving the flogger plenty of space and offering them all a good view. And then, with all his might, he brought down the first blow.

A stick that length generated quite some force. The first strike reached right across the top of the prisoner's shoulders. As the first blow landed, he instinctively recoiled, arching his back and shoulders and let out a piercing scream. The leather straps were drawn back across the skin, ripping and tearing as the sharp bones dragged their way out of his flesh. Dismas retched and his body began to shake.

That first strike was met with cheers and shouts from the soldiers, which brought a wide grin to the face of Erastus. They had been looking forward to this. The second blow landed, met with even louder cheers.

Erastus was skilled in his task and took pride in carrying it out fully. He stood to the side of the prisoner, so that the whip would land laterally across the body. With a high degree of accuracy, each strike would be made lower than the previous one, working down the prisoner's back, starting with a blow across the top of the shoulders, ending with the last one across the back of the knees. He made sure it took exactly ten blows to get that far.

By the time the back of the knees were struck, the welts were already developing where the punishment had started, at the top of the prisoner's shoulders and back, his body responding to the metal and bone that was woven into the whip straps. As the tenth blow hit with full force across the back of his legs, the prisoner fell to his knees. There were more cheers and encouragements from the onlookers, as two guards grabbed him and pulled him back to his feet, shouting at him to stay standing.

This was the cue for Erastus to raise his whip to start over at the top of the man's back, again working his way down the body. This time, the leather straps were lashing against raw flesh, the inset fragments of bone and metal driving and dragging deeper.

By the third round of lashes the skin on his back was shredded. Erastus now took half a step closer to the victim, so that the whip would wrap around his side, tearing the flesh on his chest and abdomen.

Half-way through the fourth round the prisoner fell to his knees at the foot of the post, unable to bear the savagery anymore. The last few blows all fell on his back and shoulders.

All the guards had enjoyed this spectacle, laughing, mocking, baying for more, even though Erastus did not need the encouragement. But at the end, when the victim found the strength to get back up to his feet, the guard's face changed.

'He wants some more!' the crowd was shouting.

This was a challenge to Erastus. He had been revelling in the gruesome task, but this prisoner's resilience was now riling him, goading him to dish out more punishment. This was his pride at stake. No one should be left standing when he was handing out a flogging.

Condemned by the Law

With his face reddened and his thick neck bulging and pulsating, Erastus lifted the whip again and brought it down with as much force as he could muster. The prisoner's body shuddered. As he lifted his striking arm again, the commander stepped forward and put his hand on the guard's shoulder.

'Erastus, stop now.'

'But he's still standing,' spluttered Erastus.

'He's been whipped to ribbons. Pilate may need to see him again. And he has to stay alive until we get him nailed to his tree.'

The commander had given the order. It was enough. It was meant to be thirty-nine strikes, but no one had been keeping count.

The spectacle was over and the crowd of guards sauntered off, patting Erastus on the shoulder as they left, congratulating him on a job well done. They had enjoyed their morning's entertainment. Some were muttering, surprised that the prisoner was still able to stand at the end.

One guard collected the robe that had been discarded in the dirt and threw it loosely over the man's body. He was then left standing in the centre of the courtyard, his arms still wrapped around the post, with a few remaining guards watching over him.

Dismas had been completely engrossed by this gruesome episode. Eventually he looked away from the sorry sight and slumped down in the dirt, lost in the horror, the images that he would never be able to forget echoing around his mind.

He was oblivious to the comings and goings in the courtyard over the next hour, consumed with the fear that this sort of torture was awaiting all prisoners. He had heard the many myths on the street about the Romans' appetite for torture. *How would I be able to survive a flogging like this when it comes to my turn?*

Chapter 11
The Cross

Christ redeemed us from the curse of the law by becoming a curse for us, for it is written: 'Cursed is everyone who is hung on a tree.' He redeemed us in order that the blessing given to Abraham might come to the Gentiles through Christ Jesus, so that by faith we might receive the promise of the Spirit. (Galatians 3:13-14)

The sun rose higher over the prison wall and lit up the courtyard with a soft orange glow. Following the dawn flogging, the jail's daily routine was set to begin. A commander stepped out from a doorway and the other guards looked across immediately to focus on what was about to be decreed.

'Get Jesus the Nazarene ready for execution,' and he pointed to the bloodied man who had been separated from the flogging post and was now kneeling in the dust, his hands tied loosely in front of him with a rope. 'And bring those other two rebels with him.'

The name of Jesus meant nothing to Dismas. He noted it, but had no recollection of who this man was or why the Roman guards were treating him like this.

On this command the guards jumped into action and four of them strode across the courtyard towards the cell door in front of Dismas. Inside the cell, the prisoners' usual response was to edge towards the back wall, to be out of the eyeline of the guards as they entered.

Dismas had neither the energy nor the desire to move away. He was resigned to the fact that he was a worthless street wretch, condemned to death for stealing. His time would be soon, so it may as well be now. He just remained where he was, crouched in the dirt by the door.

'Two more of you are going to die today,' barked one of the guards as they threw open the cell door and burst in.

'You can die alongside your rebel leader!' said another as he grabbed Dismas, bound his wrists with rope and dragged him out of the cell door and into the courtyard.

Dismas had no strength to argue or struggle. His time had come and whatever minor injustice was being played out did not matter. He stood in the dust, squinting in the light, hoping that his flogging would be nothing like the one he had just witnessed.

Two other guards followed behind, dragging another prisoner from the cells. It was Gestas, one of his eyes swollen shut and with purple, grey and yellow patches across his face from when he had been beaten by the other prisoners.

The two of them squinted in the brightness of the prison courtyard. As their eyes adjusted, they looked at each other, neither of them capable of speaking, but a look of terror covered Gestas' face. The two of them were equally resigned to their fate.

Dismas looked across to the mess that was Jesus. The man's robes were no longer white, but brown from the dirt and red from the blood that was seeping from his wounds. Where his robe hung loosely down over one shoulder, Dismas could see torn flesh, veins and bone. He was kneeling still and quiet, almost trance-like, his lips moving rapidly as though talking silently to himself.

Dismas and Gestas were shuffled over towards Jesus and ordered to stand next to him, where the ground was splattered with his blood.

'These other two don't need the whip,' the commander announced. 'The Jew has taken enough for them both today.'

Dismas felt a relief that he had escaped the flogging. He looked at Jesus suspiciously and a little fearfully. *This Jesus must have been especially bad to deserve that extra punishment.*

'You three are for the cross,' instructed a guard. 'Now each of you pick up one of these beams.'

Jesus was dragged to his feet by a guard, and each prisoner was nudged and pushed in the direction of three solid beams of wood that were leaning up against the prison wall next to the gates. It was a part of the cruelty of the Romans that the convicted would have to carry their own cross beam to the place of execution.

Dismas had seen many others walk through the streets carrying their crosses and had always feared that one day he would be doing it too.

In turn, each of the three convicts took the weight of the beam off the wall and on to their shoulders, Jesus shuffling forward and taking his last.

'Let's go!'

They edged towards the gates that would lead them out through the city streets. Jesus went out at the head of this grizzly procession. The beam felt heavy and painful enough on the shoulders of the two young criminals, but on Jesus it was burying into raw flesh.

'Quickly!' The guards pushed and shoved to try to get them all moving along a little faster.

Dismas knew the route well from this jail to the nearest city gates, but beyond that was new territory to him.

On the streets outside the gates he could sense the atmosphere rapidly change. Tension seemed heightened and the guards were being extra vigilant, clearly on edge. There were more of them than usual for a crucifixion procession. Normally people would step out of the way, looking on at the convicts in disgust or spitting at them. But today the crowds were pushing and shoving, following them along their route in a procession. Some women were crying and howling as they saw the sight, calling out to Jesus. Others on the street were hurling abuse at him, taunting him, waves of hatred emanating from the crowds. None of the onlookers even noticed the other two criminals following along behind.

Dismas found his respect for Jesus was growing. He had just witnessed the horrific flogging and could see he was using every last bit of his strength, determined to carry his cross. He was trudging along the route, staring ahead, with the mass of thorns still on his head, his robes hanging off him like filthy rags, barely covering his dignity.

With every step Jesus was looking weaker. Each time he stumbled the guards would shout and prod him with their spear shafts. As they approached the city gates, Jesus fell to his knees, dropping his beam. He was exhausted. There was no way he was going to be able to make it up the hill.

'We'll finish him off here then,' said a guard, as he drew his sword ready to take decisive action.

Dismas was expecting this to be the end of Jesus.

'Wait,' shouted the commander. 'We have orders to crucify him.'

The guard with his sword drawn, turned to the crowd and pointed his sword at the throat of a bystander.

'You. Pick up his beam!'

The crowd fell silent and for a moment the man looked bewildered. He slowly raised his hand and moved the sword to one side, then stepped forward from the crowd towards Jesus and placed his hand on Jesus' shoulder.

'Let me help you,' the man said.

'Be quick,' shouted the guard. They were nervous that the procession had stopped moving, leaving them vulnerable here.

The man from the crowd helped Jesus back to his feet, picked up the wooden beam and placed it on his own shoulders. The two of them began to walk side by side as the column shuffled off again.

As this grim procession passed through the city gates, Dismas realised that this was the first time he had ever been outside the walls. In his whole life, only on his final day was he now leaving the city and venturing the furthest away from his home.

He stole a glance back at the gates, seeing them for the first time from the outside. He felt no sense of loss in leaving the city. Jerusalem had not looked after him well. He owed it nothing. There was a pang of regret in his heart, that he had never been brave enough to venture away before. *Maybe my life would have been worth something if I had ever escaped the city?*

On the route beyond the gates the crowd thinned. The procession followed a dusty track, down from the city walls to the bottom of a valley, then trudged up the hill on the other side. The track was lined with tents and awnings, and the donkeys and camels, tied up next to their owner's makeshift accommodation, turned their heads to stare as they tramped past. This was where the thousands of visitors would stay during Passover week. Towards the top of the hill they passed the eerie rocks that gave this hill its name: Golgotha.

When they arrived at a clearing at the top of the hill, they found a small party of Romans already there, preparing the execution site, with the wooden posts already fixed in the ground. Scattered around them was the evidence from many years of executions, with large patches of dust on the ground, stained dark with blood. The hilltop was littered with discarded rags, bones, bent nails and even a corpse lying contorted at the edge of the clearing. There was an eerie atmosphere; the air was still and putrid.

'Drop your beams,' a soldier broke the silence, causing the crows to flap up from their feasting on the carcass, with a cawing and cackling as though they were announcing the start of the day's executions. They circled overhead. This was the place where it was to happen. This was it. This was where his life would end.

The three prisoners were ordered to lie down on the ground with their arms laid across the beams they had carried, the palms of their hands facing upwards towards the early morning sky.

As a crowd of followers slowly gathered at the top of the hill, there began a gentle chorus of discordant wailing, weeping and mourning. Soon this was accompanied by shouting and taunting from an increasingly raucous crowd.

'Keep back,' the guards kept shouting at them. They were agitated with too many people here and they could not risk the prisoners being liberated. The chanting and heckling was increasing. For a reason unknown to Dismas, many in the crowd clearly wanted to see Jesus crucified.

A guard stepped forward carrying a hammer and a handful of metal spikes, each one about the length of a man's hand. He went to Jesus first; one guard held his right hand down as another took the nail, held it to his wrist and hammered it through. It took seven or eight blows before he was happy it would hold. They moved along the beam to his other arm, pulled it taut and repeated the hammering into his left wrist. As they did so, Jesus turned his face away.

Dismas was next. As the spike was forced through his wrist, he felt his hand and fingers lock, unable to move. The pain was immense. Nausea overwhelmed him. Panic and fear flooded him. He tried to scream but no sound would come out of him. With every blow to the head of the metal spike, his body recoiled. Once one was done, the second terrorised him even more. With the third or fourth blow, the hammer caught the edge of the spike, landing on the palm of his hand. The force sent a shockwave of pain through his body as the guard cursed under his breath.

'It is in far enough, it will hold. I'm not wasting another nail on him.' The nail was left bent over, just enough of it in the wood to hold him fast.

When it was finished, the soldiers moved on. Dismas lay there in shock for a few moments, until he was brought to by another hammering sound, followed by an intense guttural scream. It was Gestas. The torrent of horrifying screams continued until the hammering finally stopped.

For a few short moments of stillness, the pain subsided, while the soldiers gathered in a small group and took some water.

Now refreshed, four soldiers approached Jesus, two on each end of the beam, and lifted it up, leaving the prisoner's feet dragging on the ground. They pulled it backwards towards the post that was already firmly planted. Standing on two small platforms, one either side of the post, they lifted the prisoner as high as they could. As they did this, Jesus' body sagged, with all his weight being taken on the spikes through his wrists. The cross beam dropped with a jolt into position near the top of the post and the soldiers hammered in a nail to hold it firmly in place. Each blow of the hammer caused a shudder of pain through the victim's body. His face contorted with agony.

They then took his feet and placed one on top of the other in front of the post. Lifting up his feet to ensure his legs were slightly bent at the knee, they took another metal spike and drove it through the top of the front foot, through the foot behind and into the wooden post, to hold the feet firm.

The four soldiers looked across at their next task and stepped towards Dismas. He knew what was coming. They dragged him towards a post to the right of Jesus and he was lifted up into position. He felt his shoulders being wrenched out of their sockets by his own body weight. The pain was unlike anything he had known before. Every blow to the nail that bored through his feet sent a shockwave throughout his body from every nerve, sinew and muscle.

The same ordeal followed for the third man, hanging him on a post to the left of Jesus. Gestas did not suffer his turn silently, making sure that every hammer blow was accompanied by a haunting shriek. All the time the crowd were jostling and baying, edging forward, guards positioned around the hilltop, pointing their spears and shouting at them all to stay back.

For the three of them their fate was sealed. There was no escape from the punishment now. The guards completed the task by approaching each prisoner and tearing off what was left of their clothing, leaving them naked and exposed, their shame complete as each of them hung on their cross.

The pain was a distraction. For each man, his entire weight was pulling down on his chest making it impossible to breathe. To get air into their bodies, they needed to shift their bodyweight from the wrists to the feet and back again. To take a breath, they had to push down on their feet to raise their body a little, allowing their lungs the freedom to empty. After pushing up with their feet and breathing out, they could breathe in and relax downwards. They would then be holding their breath until the oncoming threat of suffocation would force them to push through the immense pain, again and again. Each of them had to endure it to fulfil the instinct to take a breath, however difficult it was.

Dismas was devoid of any hope. He could only focus on developing a rhythm of breathing, accepting the pain. With each breath the pain increased, as the spikes in his wrists and feet began to tear through the flesh until they were scraping against bone.

In the simple act of taking a breath, his back was rising and falling against the bare, rough wood of the crucifix. He thought of Jesus, whose back was already one large open wound after the flogging. He looked across and saw that Jesus was barely recognisable as a man. It was only the outline shape of his body that gave any clue to his humanity.

The heat of the day was increasing and the flies were gathering, as the spilled blood attracted them to this gruesome spectacle. There was no way for the victims to swat them away as they settled and feasted. The smell of blood and death was overpowering.

Swallows swooped and danced through the air around the scene, feasting on the swarming flies.

Dismas could turn his head to the left to see Jesus, with Gestas just beyond. As he looked across to Jesus their eyes met. With his humanity stripped away and in the depths of suffering and humiliation, Jesus had every right to be full of bitterness. But instead his eyes offered a very different emotion. Dismas could see an intensity of compassion in Jesus' eyes. They spoke of kindness and empathy. *How can a man in this desperate situation still appear to be so caring?*

Beneath Jesus was a large group of followers all witnessing his absolute humiliation, all sharing in his pain. Many were crying. One woman appeared to be especially distraught.

Jesus looked down at her and said, 'Woman, here is your son.' Then to the man beside her, he said, 'Here is your mother.'

The idea that Jesus was thinking of others in the midst of his suffering, handing over the care of his mother like this, impacted Dismas' thoughts. *I am so grateful that there is no one present to witness my own end, my failure and death.*

Some in the crowd cried out to Jesus as Rabbi, some called him the Messiah, others called him brother. They were faithfully clinging on to the belief that he was still their leader, despite him being nailed to a cross.

Many were wailing as if in mourning, ripping their clothes, with tears of sorrow streaming down their faces. Dismas could not fathom why this Jesus was there alongside two thieves. These people clearly loved him. He was somebody. They respected him as a holy man. *So why is he here?*

Expecting it to have been quicker, the guards were disturbed that Jesus was still surviving. The flogging handed out earlier should have been enough to kill a man, but he was still fighting on. They began to taunt him in front of his followers.

The guard called Erastus, the one who had flogged Jesus, picked up an old broken wooden plank and, with a rusty metal spike, scratched on it some words.

'This is Jesus, King of the Jews,' he shouted as he climbed the platform to the side of the cross and nailed it above Jesus' head. 'Look at him now, nailed to a tree, next to this other scum.'

This brought a loud cheer from all the guards and some in the crowd, followed by much heckling and laughter. Erastus was enjoying the limelight, so he turned to the crowd and started to rouse them more, stirring up hostility and hatred. Parts of the crowd seemed possessed, baying for blood and death. Hissing and growling, spitting poison like a venomous snake.

Passers-by were deriding Jesus, hurling insults and curses. Priests were shouting, 'He calls himself the Messiah but can't even save himself!'

To one side, the soldiers were playing dice to win the robes that had been stripped from Jesus' body, wanting a souvenir from the day.

Dismas watched as, with immense effort, Jesus pushed himself up as high as he could to take a large breath. He lifted his face up to look directly at Erastus and spoke.

'Father, forgive them, for they do not know what they are doing.'

His body slumped and his face fell down to face the dust. The guard Erastus stood still and quiet, staring up at Jesus. Dismas was astounded. *How could Jesus ever think that the Romans deserve forgiveness, when they are inflicting all of this pain on us? Why did the priests want him dead, when the sign said he was their king?*

During these first three hours, the scene was chaotic and vicious, all of it aimed at Jesus. As time went on, the crowd started to grow tired of this sport and some began to saunter away. There was only going to be one outcome. They had seen enough and there was a Passover celebration to prepare for.

The atmosphere began to calm down, interrupted by the sobs and moans from the onlookers, along with the howls and whines from Gestas, whilst Jesus and Dismas remained mostly silent, lost in the depths of their own tortures.

Gestas continued to be true to his name. He had been groaning and screaming with the pain. His only relief seemed to be when Jesus was being taunted and mocked, which distracted him from his own suffering. Gestas joined in with the crowds, repeating their insults, mocking in as loud a mutter as he could manage. It gave him a brief respite, to focus on someone else who was going through a worse experience than him. Every last person, even Gestas, was getting some benefit from Jesus' misfortune.

Dismas' mind was in turmoil, his thoughts confused and racing. In the moment he found himself following the crowd, as he had done all his life, echoing in his thoughts the insults that were being hurled at Jesus. It had always been his habit to follow, rather than stand out in a crowd. He hated himself for the weakness.

Jesus turned his head to the right and their eyes met again. His eyes were the only part of this man that appeared to have survived the Romans' tortures. They were startlingly white, surrounded by the dirty red background of his beaten and distorted face. The vibrant brown iris in each eye showed no sign of dullness.

That look from Jesus was piercing, somehow full of compassion. He had seen this look from only one person before and she had been snatched from him. Dismas was mesmerised. He knew there had to be some truth here. *Perhaps there was hope that Jesus would be rescued by his God?* Sympathy rose in Dismas. Someone else had it worse than he did.

Whatever Jesus had done or said, he did not deserve this sort of torment and humiliation. There was no obvious crime committed other than an accusation of being their Messiah. This had no relevance at all for Dismas and certainly should not be a reason to be killed.

If anyone deserved to be treated this way, it was himself and Gestas. They were the worthless ones. The ones who had spent years stealing and thieving. No one would miss them when they were gone. No one was standing at the foot of their crosses to mourn and weep. Jesus appeared to have family, followers, people who believed in him as a Rabbi, a teacher, their Messiah. They called him their Saviour and he had a purpose.

Dismas had no idea if Jesus really was any of these things, but that look that Jesus offered spoke deeply into his soul, and his heart began to stir.

Amongst his complaining, Dismas heard Gestas copying more of the insults from the crowd.

'So if you are the Messiah they say you are, then save yourself and save us as well.'

Just like Gestas, to think of himself. Dismas felt his own mind return, knowing that this mocking was not right.

He mustered all the strength he could. As he pushed himself up with his feet to exhale, through the pain, in a whispered screech, he spoke out to Gestas.

'For once can't you see the truth?'

He then inhaled fresh air into his lungs, as his body sagged. Again, he pushed himself up and said, 'Don't you fear even God?' and he slumped back down.

Dismas was unsure if Gestas had even heard these words. As he spoke them out loud, he knew that he was also saying them to himself. He had never known or feared any God.

With the next few short, painful breaths, as loud as he could, he managed to say, 'We have the same death facing us. We deserve it more. He has done nothing to deserve this. He has done nothing wrong.'

And he collapsed, exhausted.

For the first time in his life, Dismas had declared words from his heart. He felt convicted by this violation of justice, and he spoke it out.

Jesus turned his head again to the right, to face Dismas, and their eyes met once more. Dismas had strength for one more sentence. As he looked into the eyes of Jesus, he heard himself pushing out his last words.

'Remember me when you get to your heaven.'

Jesus pushed up with his feet. As he exhaled, he breathlessly said to Dismas, 'I tell you the truth. Today you will be with me in paradise.'

*

Three hours had passed. The noon sun, which should have been glaring down on them, was weakened behind a darkening sky. Storm clouds approached from the south, rolling above the city and over the walls, as though Jerusalem itself was sending its curses over Golgotha. The crowd had mostly dissipated, with a few of Jesus' loyal followers and family remaining, including the woman who Dismas thought to be his mother.

In the growing silence, Jesus had an air of calmness. His body was crushed, but somehow He looked resolute, measured and in control. There was no fear or anger in his eyes and to Dismas he seemed immense. He found himself watching Jesus' last hours, gaining a respect for him in these strangest of circumstances. He wanted to trust and believe the promise that Jesus had made, clutching at this last morsel of hope. He wanted to believe that only a God could behave like this. That Jesus must be the Messiah that his followers believed he was.

Dismas had got into a rhythm of breathing in the first hours on the cross, but exhaustion began to creep up fast. As the hours went by, every breath became more laborious and shallower. Speech was no longer possible. Even Gestas could only manage quiet moaning and groaning to help him through the agony. They had become numb to the pain, using every effort to just maintain the breath in their bodies.

He looked out beyond the onlookers, at the landscape back towards the city. Down the hill, he noticed that the track they had ascended was lined with tamarisk trees. He remembered how he used to marvel at their beauty from inside the city. Their flowers again displaying a grace that seemed so incongruent to his own situation.

The anguish and torment of crucifixion was absolute. The physical pain in their limbs was matched by the agony of dehydration and the fever that had set in. Their bodies lacked fresh breath. Without it, the gasses trapped in their lungs were poisoning them.

Dismas could feel his heart pounding in his chest as if it wanted to escape. His temples were thumping out an irregular pattern, signalling that the end was probably close.

It was mid-afternoon as their sixth hour on the cross approached. The superstitious guards were getting anxious, unsettled by the darkened sky and chilled by the wind that was now swirling around the hilltop. Their orders were to get it completed today and to make sure the three men were dead. The city was busy with the Jewish festival and they were needed inside the walls tonight. It was time for them to end it.

'Right,' eventually came the order from the commander. 'Let's get this finished now.'

There was a resurgence of wailing from the onlookers as all the guards stirred into action.

One picked up a heavy wooden club, designed to snap bones, and he stepped towards the cross in the middle. As they approached Jesus they paused. Jesus lifted his face upwards towards heaven and pushed up with his feet to take a breath. As his body descended, he shouted out, 'My God, my God, why have you forsaken me?'

The words echoed around the hilltop.

At this exact moment, from across the valley came the almighty sound of the temple shofars. They called out from the city walls, proclaiming the ninth hour of the day, the time of the temple sacrifice. Jesus raised his eyes to the heavens and whispered, 'It is finished.'

His final breath left his body.

As the last note from the horns evaporated across the valley, Dismas noticed the quiet and the dark. Darkness had struck. Cicadas had stopped their incessant clicking, birds had stopped singing, the swallows had stopped swooping as the flies had retreated. Dismas was confused. *Is it still the daytime?* In his delirious state he did not know the time of day or how long he had been hanging there.

The sobbing from onlookers and family broke the eerie silence. Some fell to their knees distraught. Others just looked disappointed, shrugged and turned their faces away from the dead and defeated Jesus. *Maybe they were expecting more?* Some of the well-fed religious-looking types seemed to be pleased that Jesus was dead. They turned on their heel and bounded back towards the city.

Jesus' mother sank to her knees, her cheeks wet with tears, her face turned towards heaven and hands clasped in front of her. The look on her face told the story of her heartbreak. As she muttered some words heavenwards, she and those around her began tearing their clothes. They were grieving the loss of a loved son and brother.

The cold, dark silence that had fallen across the land was spooking the guards. One of them took his spear and forced it into the side of Jesus' body. They needed to make sure he was dead. As he pushed the spear in there was a release of air and water from the flesh, but no flinch from the body. He was dead.

'He's gone.'

'We need to finish off the other two,' and they stepped towards Dismas' cross.

Terror rampaged through his mind. He had arrived at the point of death. He was helpless. He could do nothing to express his torment physically, but the fear behind his eyes was manifest. Part of him wanted it to happen, to release him from this torture, whilst he also felt a terror for what may come next. Either way, logic and clear thinking had long given way to instinct.

He heard the dull thud of the club on flesh and the snap of bones breaking. One strike and his legs were splintered. It took a few seconds before he realised it was his legs that had been struck. Dismas' whole body slumped, hanging from his arms as his shattered lower legs were no longer able to bear his weight. It forced him to exhale all his breath.

He was numb to the pain but the inability to draw any air into his lungs sent a message of panic through his whole being. His limbs twitched in a futile attempt to lift himself up, but had no effect on his broken body. He tried speech but no sound would come. All that was released from his parched mouth was a splutter of blood. His chest felt as though it would burst with the pain. If anyone had noticed, they would have seen his eyes widen, terror and fear consuming his mind.

Within a few moments, starved of breath, life departed his body.

Chapter 12
Restored

*Instead of their shame my people will receive a double portion,
and instead of disgrace they will rejoice in their inheritance; and
so they will inherit a double portion in their land, and everlasting
joy will be theirs.* (Isaiah 61:7)

Habib opened his eyes. He was still lying on the warm grass, next to the blue plinth. Jesus was back, sitting alongside, watching over him.

'You remember it all so clearly, don't you?'

His words revived Habib from his memories. He did remember every moment. What had happened was still so lucid to him. He knew that it had been so painful, but he could no longer feel the pain. He did have a full understanding that there had been unspeakable agony.

'Yes.'

'There is comfort here. Comfort and rest from the bad things endured on earth. Relief from the pain.'

Jesus stood up, held out his hand and pulled Habib to his feet from his resting place.

'Come. Let's walk for a while.'

They walked side by side, in silence, sauntering slowly to the edge of the clearing and back through the woodland, Habib still caught up in the memories of his death. The trauma and pain had left him, but he knew all that had happened.

'I didn't think that pain like that was possible,' Habib said. Having shared the experience with Jesus, he felt he would have a good understanding.

'Only you can appreciate the physical pain of the cross. But that was not my real pain.' Jesus paused to let the words settle. 'My true suffering was like yours. I was alone for the only time in my life.'

Habib was puzzled. He thought back to the scene on that hillside outside Jerusalem. He remembered the crowd at the foot of Jesus' cross, his family and followers. He remembered the woman who he thought was Jesus' mother.

'Who was that woman? The one who was there when you were on the cross, who stayed there to the end.'

Jesus smiled. He knew which woman he was talking about.

'She is so precious,' and his smile broadened at the thought of her. 'She is a woman of perfect faith, who did everything that the Father asked of her. She knew what would happen even though it caused her great pain. She is under someone else's good care for now and she will be here when the time is right.'

'So is that why you felt so alone?' Habib was feeling a little braver. 'You were leaving her.'

'In part, yes. That was difficult. I would love for us to be together again. But when I died on that cross, I was separated from my Father and my Spirit for the first time. For me, to be apart from them was a pain like no other.'

Habib paused, lost in his thoughts for a moment. *Why would they abandon him like that, at the time when he needed them the most? It* made him ponder his own situation. His separation from his mother and father since the moment of his birth. Tears welled up in his eyes, blurring his vision. He wanted to let it all out. To scream and shout and sob away all the anger and hurt and sorrow that had been stored up inside him over all those years. He felt an arm around his shoulders as Jesus comforted him.

'We will ease it out slowly. There is no hurry.'

The emotion subsided and Habib began to see more clearly now, the flowers on the forest floor filling his vision with colour, and their rich scent reviving him to the present. They walked on a bit further. Jesus continued.

'What you went through on the cross was not in vain. What happened to you will be remembered by the world for ever.'

Habib had no concept as to how or why this would be, but the news warmed his soul. For the first time in his life, he felt a little bit proud at the thought of having done something useful. He stopped to look at a flower.

'Why did you rescue me?'

Jesus took a step towards Habib and put his hand on his shoulder.

'You were orphaned and alone. You are so precious to Father who created you. Father does not abandon his children.'

Habib needed to delve into the depths of this truth to fully understand it. He paused, his hand touching the flower that captivated him; its petals of blue, purple and pink danced in his hand, as though being tickled. The concept that he had never been abandoned, never been alone, was a difficult one to grasp. He wanted to be honest with Jesus.

'But I did feel abandoned. If God was there . . .' and his voice faded away as he tried to process his thoughts. 'But I failed your Father in my life. I did many bad things. I was filthy and dirty and unclean. I could not have been further away from God.'

'We know that's how you felt. We felt it too. I walked in your footsteps. I have lived your story and I know your heart.'

'But I have never done anything for you, or even for anyone.'

'That is not how love works,' and Jesus turned to face Habib, looking directly into his eyes. 'It is not about what you have done, it is about who you are. We love you because you are a child of God.'

Habib paused, as this truth plunged deep into his heart.

'I have never loved anyone. How could anyone love me back?' Habib looked down to the ground, not being able to meet Jesus' gaze.

'You have been loved by many and you have loved too. I have not forgotten the love that you showed to Riha. I saw how you cared for her. You brought her happiness and protection. When she died you watched over her and proved how much you loved her.'

At the very mention of her name, hope burst into his heart. That unrecognised kernel of love that he had felt so many years ago, exploded inside him and flooded his body. He began to comprehend the potential power of love. He was quiet again for a few moments, wallowing in this new-found emotion that was growing inside him.

They carried on walking and reached the edge of the woodland. As the trees cleared, there before them was a broad grassy plain, stretching to the horizon where it met mountains. Walking towards them along the edge of the woodland was a group of thirty or forty children, chattering and laughing. In their midst, Habib recognised the woman that was looking after them. It was the Holy Spirit, now a radiant woman, carrying a baby in her arms as a mother would, encouraging and nurturing the children around her.

As the two men walked and talked across the plain, the children caught up with them and strolled alongside, listening to every word, dancing, skipping, surrounding them with joy and happiness.

One child took Habib's hand as they walked. It took him by surprise and his first instinct was to pull away. Contact with anyone, especially other children, was not natural to him. He looked down into the smiling face of a little girl. She had such a depth of love in her eyes that he could only relax and let her take hold of his hand. His nervousness subsided and he found himself gripping that hand as tightly as he dared.

'Who are these children?' asked Habib.

'These children are so special,' answered Jesus. 'In all of their faces you will see the face of the Father. They are the young ones, who came here early. They are still blossoming and maturing. They are all adopted too, like you, but growing up in heaven, in our care.'

Habib felt his heart was going to burst with the compassion of Jesus.

As they walked together, Habib looked up and suddenly stopped mid-stride. Across the plain he saw a tamarisk tree, rising out of the grassland, towering proudly over the landscape, in full bloom, as tall and broad as the temple. The largest and most perfectly shaped tamarisk tree he could have imagined, bejewelled with pink blossoms that were shimmering and glistening in the light.

'I remember seeing those trees,' he said thoughtfully out loud. 'There was something about them that always seemed to hold my gaze.'

'That's Abraham's tamarisk tree,' responded Jesus with a knowing look. 'He planted it a long time ago for the generations to come. It grows here now, a symbol of Father's promised land. A symbol of peace to all past and future generations. A promise that a long-lasting peace will come for everyone who believes.'

As they ambled closer to the tree, Habib remembered his early days, on his own in the city, gazing at the tamarisk trees. Back then he rejected that feeling of peace. He would not allow it to enter his heart, thinking that it would only lead to pain and disappointment. Now he felt fully able to receive it.

'What about the others?'

'Who do you mean?'

'What will happen to the others? My family, the people I knew . . .' his voice trailed off. He took a deep breath. 'What I mean is the people who threw me out, spat at me, rejected me, hurt me. The ones who may not be here.'

'They are not for you to worry about. They all have their own story and their own reasons. The Father's love is deeper than you can imagine. He will cover them if they want it.'

'Most of them I don't want to see again. Some of them will want to hurt me – or worse.' Habib could not help himself. There was still a trace of fear troubling him.

'You are safe here. This is a safe place. The safest of places. There is no harm or hurt any more. Just trust.'

Despite all he had seen, heard and felt since he had been in heaven, Habib still struggled to adjust his innermost thoughts and instincts that had been developed and honed throughout his life on the streets.

Seeing this, Jesus said, 'Let me explain. For you to understand who you are and why you are here in heaven, it will help if you understand my journey.'

Habib had that familiar puzzled look on his face once again.

They settled down to rest on the grass under the cover of Abraham's tamarisk tree. The children settled down too, dotted around Jesus, transfixed by every word that he spoke. The Holy Spirit was seated amongst the children, attending to them, holding a hand or stroking a little girl's long hair. They were all a picture of perfection.

'It was never the intention that you would live that difficult life. It pains us to see any suffering.' Jesus looked directly into Habib's eyes. 'Our love for you knows no boundaries. We adore you. The measure of our love for you is so great that it needed the biggest demonstration of that love that we could comprehend, to be able to rescue you.

'That is why I was hanging on that cross next to you. I chose to take your pain and suffering, your torture and torment. Everyone's. I took that all with me to my cross. I was separated from my Father and my Spirit for the only time. With all that filth and pain and sin pinned to the cross with me, they could no longer be in my presence.

'More than that, I died. After my death I returned to earth to see my family and followers, so that they could tell everyone that even death has been beaten. Death is not the end, but a start. I died on earth so that you could have eternal life in heaven.

'In this way I was able to release you from all of your sin and death, so that you too can now be in the presence of God the Father. You are now cleansed and pure, just as we made you and intended you to be. We are so desperate for you to be restored to our family.

'You are worth everything to us. Whatever you have done, thought or said, we can forgive you. You are not cursed. You are not condemned. You can look me in the eye and know your immense value to us.

'I know what it was like for you to be rejected and separated from the love of your family. I know what your emptiness and loneliness felt like. I learned what it is like to be tempted. I understand what it is like to be a man. And I overcame it all so that you can too.'

Jesus smiled, with so much love in his eyes.

'Habib. My beloved. You know more than anyone what had to be suffered physically on the cross. I am so sorry you had to endure that. You suffered it well. You are now heaven's witness to it.'

Every sound ceased. Every child was still, looking intently at Habib. All of heaven held its breath. The whole of creation paused as these words permeated Habib to his essence.

Habib had only ever believed that he was worth nothing, with no purpose. With this declaration from Jesus, he now knew he was worth everything, with an eternal purpose.

Slowly the sounds and movements of heaven ebbed back into Habib's consciousness.

The Holy Spirit rose from amongst the children, who had all been so engrossed in this special moment. In her hands she was carrying a wooden bowl. She stepped forward towards Jesus and settled back down at his feet.

Habib could pick up a scent from the bowl, the aroma of the sweetest of perfumes. In the bowl was an amber-coloured liquid with a fragrance that brought back memories of the perfume sellers in the markets of Jerusalem.

She cupped the perfume in her hands and held it over Jesus' feet, allowing it to trickle through her fingers. His feet began to glisten, making the scars show more clearly than ever. She then leaned forward, took her long hair in her hands and began to wipe his feet with her hair. The fragrance of the perfume filled the air around them as this act of worship played out before them all.

Jesus gave her a briefest of signals with his hand and she stood, holding the bowl with what was left of the perfume in it. She took a drop of this precious oil on her finger and went around the group of children, anointing each of them on the forehead. Each child was radiant as they received this blessing.

Lastly, she came to Habib and knelt down beside him. Wide-eyed, Habib looked at the Holy Spirit as she was gazing adoringly back at him, a mother's gaze so full of pride and love for her children. His heart leaped again, knowing the deep blessing of her presence. She dipped her finger into the bowl, reached across and touched his forehead with the oil.

His mind returned to that one moment of intimacy, in that filthy alleyway, when he had anointed Riha's head with oil. At the moment the Holy Spirit touched his forehead, she released something that had departed him a very long time ago. Joy came back into his heart. The Holy Spirit had revived in him her precious gift of joy. His restoration was now complete.

The fragrance of the oil filled his senses and he closed his eyes as relief overwhelmed him. He felt life, in intensity, returning to his body. He started to smile and laugh. Joy was bubbling up from within.

The children excitedly jumped to their feet and began to celebrate, singing and laughing. Habib smiled and watched as they danced around. A young girl and boy danced over in his direction, hand in hand. They both held out a hand to him.

'Join in!' they chimed. 'Dance with us!'

Cautiously Habib took their hands and rose to his feet. He had never done this before. He moved his arms up and down in time to their song, unsure how it would look. As he picked up the rhythm, his legs began to bend at the knee, bouncing his body in time to the music. He smiled at his awkwardness and his two dancing partners giggled with delight.

Finally, he let himself go. He was dancing, singing, laughing and jumping around like the other children. He was wholly taken up in the excitement, losing himself in the joy and worship.

As he danced, he looked over to Jesus who was also holding hands with some children, spinning around, lost in joy. Their eyes met and they grinned at each other.

'Thank you!' Habib called out.

Jesus responded with an ecstatic laugh.

This was Habib's first step towards being released into his purpose of a life in heaven. He was engulfed in love, living in it permanently and completely, with the reassurance and security that it brought. The only natural response he could make to all of this was to be thankful and to worship. To sing and dance with joy.

It took a long while for these celebrations to subside. Eventually the children danced away leaving Habib giddy with excitement, grinning at Jesus as he walked towards him.

'I think you are ready now,' said Jesus, taking Habib by surprise.

'Ready for what?'

'This is my return as well as yours. Your heart is mended. You are complete, as we made you to be. My work here is done for now, but I will always be here with you.'

Habib had learned now that he could trust Jesus, even though these words were mysterious to him. The confused look on his face was obvious and prompted a little more explanation.

'Everyone else knows that I am back and the victory over sin and death is won, but they have not seen me yet. The saved have had each other, whilst the lost have been alone and needed me. It has been more important to ensure you were cared for, but now that task is complete and I must go. It is time for us all to celebrate a great victory.'

Jesus turned and walked away from the tree, a short distance towards a horse. The horse was taller than any Habib had seen before, a dappled white and silvery grey colour, adorned with a bridle made of shimmering golden braid. It was led by two angels, similar to the angel that had revived Habib. These creatures amazed him; imposing and graceful, glowing with light, their wings gently floating through the air behind them.

Suddenly ten more angels appeared and attended to Jesus. They were preparing him for something special. There was excitement building in the air as they smiled and laughed whilst dressing, preening and fussing around him. He seemed to love their attentions, rewarding their affections with his own playful chatter.

They dressed him in a pure white robe, edged with golden ribbon and a golden sash over His shoulder to his waist. He had no shoes and proudly displayed on his feet and wrists the only scars in heaven. On his head they placed a crown made of light that looked solid enough to touch. Three or four strands of golden light, like ropes, were twisted together, shimmering and sparkling, with shards of light sparking off the top and sides. To Habib these looked like golden thorns, just like the last crown he had seen Jesus wear.

Jesus looked like a prince, radiating peace, purity and love with light beaming from him in all directions. Habib was in awe of him.

'I am ready,' Jesus declared. His attendants stepped back, bowed down around him and worshipped him.

The two angels who had been leading the horse, took their cloaks and lay them over the horse's back for Jesus to sit on. Then, standing one either side of Jesus, they lifted him up on to the horse.

In unison, all the angels in attendance took off into the sky, flying in all directions in a blaze of light and colour, booming out the words, 'Gather, gather, gather,' like a distant thunder rolling through the valleys.

As they departed, Habib stared skywards, the line of his gaze following them until they were out of sight. He was mesmerised by them.

When all that was left was the echo of their call to gather, he looked back down from the sky and saw that Jesus was gone.

Chapter 13
Homecoming

And he will send his angels with a loud trumpet call, and they will gather his elect from the four winds, from one end of the heavens to the other. (Matthew 24:31)

There was an atmosphere of excitement building. From some distance away Habib could hear the sound of roaring, that echoed off the surrounding hills, filling the whole kingdom. Half-way up the tallest mountain, at the head of the valley, he could see the Holy Spirit. Her form was that of a lion and on her left was a lamb. Both animals stood upright, front legs locked straight in front of them, with their chests out and heads held up high.

As the roaring grew louder, yellow, red and orange flames danced in the sky above them. The fire was surrounding them, flowing out from them in all directions. Habib noticed that there was no smoke. In flames like that the lion and the lamb should have been burned up, like a temple sacrifice, but they remained there, alive and standing proud.

The lion was creating a deep, thunderous roar, booming across the valley. A strong, rumbling, immense sound that reverberated through Habib's body.

He was enraptured, his heart racing with excitement. The Holy Spirit was not just the gentle, caring, creative, joyful being whom he had known as a companion to Jesus. The Spirit was roaring with power, proclaiming a great triumph, announcing to the heavens the victory over death, rousing everyone to attend the celebrations. This was a call to prayer that resonated with his very soul. He felt thankful. Thankful for the sacrifice that Jesus had made so that he could be here. He felt a love for Jesus growing in his heart.

Habib stepped forward towards the place where Jesus had been prepared by the angels a few moments ago. On the grass where he had stood there were traces of golden dust, sparkling in the light. Starting from this point on the ground was a narrow path of a rich blue colour, cut into the grass. It glinted a thousand shades of azure, paved with what looked like sapphire, etched with intricate swirling patterns like the designs he had seen when girls had decorated themselves with henna.

Habib began to walk along this blue path, that meandered and broadened across the meadows in front of him, in the direction of the roaring. As he walked, he saw other blue paths coming into view, running down the sides of the valley, across the plain, converging at various points up ahead. There was movement on all of them, other people following their paths, also answering this call to prayer.

A little way ahead, standing across the middle of his path, Habib saw one of the winged creatures, an angel. As he got closer and the angel came into full sight, he recognised it as the same one who had revived him when he first awoke in heaven. It was wearing the same pure white robe with golden braid and in its belt was tucked a shofar, made from what looked like a twisted horn of a sheep or goat, polished to create intricate patterns from the bronze, brown and cream colours.

Habib approached and the angel bowed his head in greeting.

'I need you to follow me now,' the angel said. The angel's voice was unlike any he had heard before. It was authoritative and clear, but the sounds it generated were made up of numerous notes and tones, resounding in unison, like the sound of a whole choir but coming from just one being.

In awe of it, Habib was only going to obey. He remembered the calming sound that the angel's wings had made when he first woke up, and he felt no fear.

They continued along the path together. Habib became curious.

'I want to say thank you for bringing me back to life here. It was you before, wasn't it, beating your wings to bring me back?'

'Yes, that was me. It has been my honour to always serve you.'

This intrigued Habib. He recalled previously how he thought he had recognised the creature.

'I've seen you before, haven't I?' not quite knowing for certain. 'Not just when you revived me, but before that.'

'Yes. When you awoke in heaven, your spirit recognised me. I have been alongside you from the moment of your first birth. When you were born I was commissioned to be with you, to watch over you. I have stood next to you through every second of your first life. My role was to protect you and keep you, so that you could fulfil the plan that the Father had purposed for you. I attended to you those last few hours on the cross and carried you through. I then had the privilege of being at your second birth, here.'

Habib was amazed. The realisation that he had never been forgotten, had always been protected and cared for every day of his life, was profound and humbling.

'It seems I have a lot more to thank you for than I had realised,' not really knowing what else to say. Then a question came to him.

'What is your name?'

The angel stopped mid stride, turned and looked down at Habib.

'I am called Shamar.' The angel smiled at Habib. Shamar was so thrilled that Habib was finally free to be able to speak out those words. This one simple question that had previously sent waves of panic through Habib. Shamar was honoured that he was the first.

'Well, thank you, Shamar. It seems you know me better than anyone. Will I get to spend more time with you now?'

'We can walk together for a while,' and Shamar reached down and took hold of Habib's hand. It looked like an adult walking alongside a small child, as they continued along the blue path together, meadows either side of them. As they walked along, the flowers turned their heads to gaze at them.

Their route took them further down the valley where now and again other paths would converge with theirs, bringing other people onto the same path. But they were ahead or behind, not too close to disturb their precious peace.

Habib felt there was no need to talk, despite hundreds of questions that were rising in his mind. He felt it right to simply enjoy being in the presence of this angel, who had shared all he had been through. Shamar understood him and he felt at peace.

The path was widening and rose in front of them to ascend a small hill. Shamar broke the silence.

'My work at your side is nearly complete. You no longer have any need for my service. You are where you belong now.'

As they reached the summit of the hill, opening up before them was a spectacle. A valley, wider than he had ever seen or imagined, was surrounded on each side by gentle hillsides. Feeding into it from all directions were blue paths, now streaming with people, all converging on the plain.

The valley floor was not the rich green colours, like the other parts of heaven he had seen. It looked mostly white, fluid, with the occasional splash of rich colours. He gasped as he realised that this valley was entirely full of people. It was a gathering of millions and millions of people, dressed mostly in white robes, with many in more colourful clothing. To Habib it looked like festival time in Jerusalem, when the city would welcome visitors from every tribe and nation of the earth.

Each person had a unique crown on their head. Some had narrow golden bands, some wider and silver, many with ornate patterns and designs etched into them. Others had coloured jewels of all shapes and sizes, embedded into the precious metal. Habib noticed many like his own, made of flowers and leaves. He lifted his hands to his head to check his garland was still resting there. As he touched it, the flowers released a fresh aroma that permeated the air all around him.

Habib and Shamar walked along their path as it led down the gentle slopes into the valley. As the path flattened out and they approached the edge of the gathering, there was a hush that came across the crowd, an anticipation.

On the horizon, at the head of the valley, in the far distance, was a mountain range. Higher than anyone could climb, broader than anyone could walk around. Above the mountains the sky became filled with thousands of angels, criss-crossing the sky in all directions, leaving trails of light and sparks in their wake.

As Shamar and Habib reached the edge of the gathering, the multitude of angels glided down to take up positions all around the edge of the valley, completely encircling the crowd.

At the foot of the mountains Habib could see a stone plinth made from one piece of lapis lazuli, much larger than the one he had been spending time on while recounting his story to Jesus. At the front edge of the plinth was the source of all the water. The spring of the life-giving water that poured from the stone, down the hillside, across the valleys, flowing through the entire landscape.

The centre of the stone was occupied by light. This light was the Father. It was the most intense, dazzling of lights, brighter than lightning in a dark night sky, yet Habib was still able to look directly at it. As he stared, his mouth fell open in absolute wonder. Light emanating from the Father swirled across the valley towards him and into him. It felt as though it was filling him, healing him, feeding him. He could sense himself standing taller. He thought to himself, '*This is me. This is who I am.*'

And here, in heaven, he knew that this was all that was needed for anyone to qualify to be here. He was accepted.

He looked up at Shamar, who was smiling at him again.

'You are ready now,' the angel announced. 'It is time for me to move on.'

'I must thank you properly. How can I possibly do that?'

'There is no need. I know already. It has been my duty and my honour to know you and serve you. It is not because of me that you are here. It is because of Jesus. In fact, I really should be thanking you. Because of you, I have been awarded a most special prerogative. I am to start these celebrations.'

Shamar knelt down and embraced Habib. In that moment they could feel the strength of fellowship that bonded them, like a transfer of energy. Peace, love and joy flowed between them, feelings that could only be shared by two beings who have spent every living moment together.

'Now step aside,' said Shamar with a huge grin.

Habib grinned back and took a step away from Shamar. He could tell this was going to be good.

As the angel crouched down, with both hands touching the ground, he began to generate a low rumbling noise.

The crowd began to murmur, punctuated with a few excited shrieks and squeals. All eyes in heaven were trained on Shamar, the catalyst of this energy, this pure anticipation. The excitement was building for what was coming next.

Every other angel around the perimeter of the valley, followed Shamar's lead and also crouched. Tens of thousands of angels, surrounding this massive crowd of people, all began to create this awesome sound.

Initially, the sound was so low it could only be felt through the ground, rumbling and reverberating. The vibrations then became audible as the sounds grew increasingly louder until it became like the sound of a thousand horses galloping, thundering into battle.

As the sound reached its peak, Shamar rose to his feet, towering over the nearby people. He extended all six of his wings as wide as they could reach. Following Shamar's lead, every other angel around the perimeter stood up in unison, spread their wings wide and reached their hands skywards. Shamar reached to his golden belt and took from it the shofar. He clasped his hands around it, brought the mouthpiece to his lips and began to blow. A trumpet sound rose from deep within him, a triumphant fanfare.

It reminded Habib of the trumpet calls he would hear from the temple at Rosh Hashanah. But this was so much more than those celebrations at the start of a new year. This was a victory call, announcing the start of a new era.

Shamar played his fanfare six times, each time getting louder and more powerful. At the end of the sixth playing, every angel took up their own shofar and joined the trumpet call for its seventh refrain. The noise was immense, a majestic announcement across the heavens. As the echo of the last note resounded up the valley, Shamar launched himself up into the sky, leaving a trail like a golden waterfall behind. Around the valley every angel did the same, each one shooting upwards, filling the sky, turning it into an effervescent golden kaleidoscope of patterns. Their radiance filled the skies, the whole of heaven resonating to the sight and sound of God's glory.

The crowd began to sparkle with excitement. The anticipation was tangible. Every few moments there was a fizz and crackle as light sparked above a section of people.

Habib loved this spectacle. He stood watching with wide eyes, taking in every detail of the display. Out of habit he was still standing towards the edge of the crowd, where he could observe it all.

Habib thought about the last time he had seen a celebration. Back then, he had been scavenging in the streets of Jerusalem alongside Riha, watching a wedding celebration pass by. She had always wanted to go to a wedding, to join in with the party. His heart was warmed to know that she was here somewhere in this crowd, enjoying the biggest and most joyous celebration there had ever been.

In all the excitement he had not considered the crowds. It dawned on him now how comfortable he felt being amongst other people. There were thousands and thousands of others here, all ages and colours. He could hear so many different languages in their singing. The children were dancing and jumping around. It was such a joy for Habib to see children out in the open, at the very centre of all these celebrations.

Feeling wholly at ease amongst the crowd, Habib wandered through, taking it all in. Someone turned to him and said, 'Welcome, it is so great to have you here.'

No stranger had ever before said words like these to him. In the past a stranger showing kindness was someone to be suspicious of, but now Habib knew that this kindness was genuine.

Someone else took a few steps towards him and embraced him. He felt shy, but had no instinct to push them away or run. Here he could let it happen. A hug from an unknown friend felt so honest and true.

A small crowd began to gather around him, patting him on the back and shoulders, saying 'welcome', 'we love you,' and 'we are so happy to have you here'. And he felt loved.

Through his tears of joy, Habib looked up and there he was: Jesus, on the white horse, looking down at him with his eyes also filled with tears. The Spirit was with him, surrounding him.

All around Jesus was light. Like the light that flowed from the Father, light poured out from the people towards Jesus, expressing their worship. Habib held up his hand to see the same light moving out from himself, flowing towards Jesus. And his tears too, as they formed in Habib's eyes, moved across to form in the eyes of Jesus. They shed the same tears of joy together. There was such profound power in this love.

The news of Jesus' arrival rippled across the valley and the huge crowd started to chatter with excitement.

'He is back!'

'He is here!'

'It is Him!'

The air above was sparking wildly, like fresh wood thrown on a hot fire at night. The rumour rumbled through the valley like wildfire.

'He is about to pronounce,' said someone nearby and a hushed silence fell over the masses. Suddenly all was still.

Jesus sat high in his saddle, surveying this wonderous gathering. He then looked down, his eyes directly meeting Habib's. With their eyes fixed on each other, in a voice like thunder rolling across the valley, he boomed to the multitudes, 'Today I am with you in paradise.'

Then followed the most immense release of celebration, an outpouring of joy and excitement, the likes of which heaven had never seen before. Cheering, shouting, whooping, dancing, jumping, chanting, laughing. Each person had their own way of glorifying Jesus' return to heaven. The heavens turned into a wild display of colour and lights, angels dancing and singing, flying across the sky in every direction.

Habib felt the joy building and a laugh coming from deep within his chest. It was not an instinctive feeling for him, but it did feel natural. He laughed out loud. Others around him started to pick up on this infectious outpouring of joy and they too burst into laughter.

People were looking at him and joining in. Following his lead. As this part of the crowd surrounding Habib was laughing, yellow and orange light in hundreds of different hues started to rise above them like flames. It filled the sky over their heads as their laughter poured out in celebration and worship.

Habib looked out at the chaos unravelling across the valley and could see pockets of different colours rising from the crowds. The cacophony of sounds and languages that filled the valley created colours that swirled and rose above the crowd. Some sections created shades of greens, some blues, some vibrant reds and purples, as everyone worshipped in their own way.

The light rose up high and flowed towards the head of the valley. As the colours merged, they formed into a brilliant white light, streaming towards the Father.

Habib could hear the intense singing from all corners of the throng. Nearby, three or four rounds of the same chorus were being sung in different languages, creating the most beautiful of harmonies. Each language complemented the others in their tone and cadence, and Habib found he could understand the words being sung.

'Holy, Holy, Holy is the Lord Almighty!'

'Glory to God in the highest heavens!'

'Blessing and honour to the Lamb on the throne!'

The words of praise and worship brought all the glory to the Father; a thousand tongues praising the name of Jesus for his victory; an outpouring of heartfelt thanksgiving.

Habib started to sing. As the melodies surrounded him, notes began to work up from deep inside himself and as he opened his mouth, words of praise came forth. Just quietly at first, but as he grew in confidence he sang in a way he never had before. To his own surprise, his voice could match the harmonies in the air around him.

He closed his eyes and any self-consciousness disappeared. He pulled back his shoulders, his chest filled with air and he began to sing out loudly, releasing joyful, heartfelt worship with words of praise unknown to him. He sang out in adoration with every part of his being.

As the music rose so did the light that it generated, creating every tone of riches. Golds, silvers, pearls and some like molten metal, all vibrant and shimmering, radiating the rejoicing from the worshippers. The colours danced through the air towards Jesus, combining with his own radiance. In return, the light from the Father ran out to meet Jesus, embracing him, edifying him, welcoming him home.

Jesus' horse began to walk slowly through the multitudes, in the direction of the mountainside at the head of the valley. People took off their cloaks and laid them down on the ground in front of him. Others laid palm leaves down to welcome him home, or even laid themselves face down in worship as he approached.

He moved through the crowd and welcomed every person individually, greeting each by name. His eyes would meet theirs accompanied by a gentle word, a smile or a loving look.

He offered the same reassuring look that he had given Habib a few moments ago. Habib had felt that love from Jesus and could see that same love being poured out for each person individually. As Jesus looked into their eyes, his became like blazing fires that burned the message of all-consuming love deep into their hearts.

Everyone had an individual response to the love of Jesus. For some it was a simple 'Thank you.' For others they needed to fall prostrate before him, offering themselves to him wholly. Some were on their knees in supplication, others were jumping up and down, bubbling over with excitement and emotions. But for all, it was an act of heartfelt worship as they were overwhelmed by his very presence.

Jesus continued to meander through the multitudes, making his way towards the head of the valley. Only when every person had been greeted did Jesus walk his horse up towards the base of the stone plinth. He dismounted and knelt down on the ground before his Father, himself in worship.

Father, the immense light, stood towering over Jesus, who was kneeling before him. He spread his arms out high and wide, for a few seconds looking like a brilliant white crucifix on the mountainside, created from beams of light rather than beams of wood. He then held his arms out to reach out to his Son, Jesus.

Jesus rose to his feet and approached the Father. He ascended the steps with his hands outstretched towards the Father. Their hands touched and the Father pulled Jesus in towards him, into an enveloping embrace. The two became a single body of light and fire and sound and emotion. Within that embrace, Habib could see the glory of the Father, the face of Jesus and the presence of the Holy Spirit. The three as one. They were power and love.

Light and sound exploded from them in a wave of energy that engulfed the valley and the heavens. Tumultuous instinctive worship rang out from all, as every angel raced across the sky, trumpeting the triumph.

Habib knew the price that had been paid for this victory, to put Jesus back on his throne in heaven. He knew he was loved. He knew he was free. Habib now knew, for the first time in his life, that he was in the right place.

The jubilee continued for some time, Habib joining in, in absolute freedom. In the midst of the celebrations, Habib heard a voice call out.

'Habib, my beloved.'

He did not react.

'Habib.'

He registered it this time and simply wondered who was being called.

'Habib.'

He heard it again and thought he recognised the voice, but could not place it.

'Habib!'

He finally realised it was him that someone was calling for. He brought his hand up to his breast pocket to check the white stone with his name on it. This was the first time he had heard his name used by anyone other than Jesus.

'Habib, my beloved.' There was a hand on his shoulder and he turned to see a sight that he never imagined would be possible.

'Habib . . . my beloved . . . I'm . . ?'

'I know who you are,' he said, so full of excitement he could barely contain his emotions. 'Ma!' he spluttered through his tears.

His mother took a step towards him and they shared the warmest, most longed-for embrace. An embrace that went all the way through him, wrapping him up entirely, completely. A most profound, life-giving embrace. In an instant all feelings of loneliness and abandonment were gone, no longer with any hold over him.

He took a small step back, to take it all in. He looked at his mother through blurred eyes. She looked just a little older than him, petite with long black hair. Her brown eyes, fixed to his, were so caring and loving. Her smile was so warm and gentle.

He had many questions but knew that his answers would all come in time. For now, though, he just had to ask one.

'Ma, how did you know my name? Jesus has only just given it to me.'

'Habib, my beloved son. That is the name I gave you from the moment you were born. That is the name I have always been using for you.'

Tears welled up from the depths of his heart. Healing tears, flowing freely down his face, putting right the years of pain and loss. Mending his broken heart. His mother reached up and wiped them from his face.

'I have so longed to do that, my precious son. I have kept a room for you in my house.'

Habib was home.

.

Postscript

Jesus is a proven historical figure, who was crucified by the Roman occupiers of Jerusalem at the insistence of the religious leaders of the day who did not agree with or accept the teachings he brought. He was executed alongside two common thieves.

This book is a work of imagination, based on this short passage from the Bible found in Luke 23.

One of the criminals who hung there hurled insults at him: 'Aren't you the Messiah? Save yourself and us!'

But the other criminal rebuked him. 'Don't you fear God,' he said, 'since you are under the same sentence? We are punished justly, for we are getting what our deeds deserve. But this man has done nothing wrong.'

Then he said, 'Jesus, remember me when you come into your kingdom.'

Jesus answered him, 'I tell you the truth, today you will be with me in paradise.' (Luke 23:39-43)

However, the teachings of Jesus are not based on imagination or fiction, but they tell the truth of who he was and is.

Some people may find it hard to believe that forgiveness of sins and salvation are that easy to achieve, often thinking that Christianity is about keeping to rules or doing good deeds. Others may feel that they are undeserving of a such an immense gift.

But there are many promises in the Bible that point us to a God who wants us to know him closely and to be with him. Two such verses from the book of Romans say:

If you declare with your mouth, 'Jesus is Lord,' and believe in your heart that God raised him from the dead, you will be saved. (Romans 10:9)

Everyone who calls on the name of the Lord will be saved. (Romans 10:13)

It is a simple act to accept Jesus as your Saviour and to know the love of God.

If this story has sparked your interest in Jesus and you would like to learn more about him and his teachings, I do encourage you to follow it up. A good way to start would be to read about the life of Jesus in the Bible. Or maybe contact your local church, to find someone who can talk to you, share the teachings of the Bible with you and help you get to know Jesus personally as your friend and Saviour.

If you have any comments or questions about the content or ideas expressed in this book, please do contact me via the website www. robseabrook.com.

Discussion Questions

This book may be a good resource to use for church book clubs, home groups or study groups for Christians, as well as people who may just be interested in learning more about the teachings of Jesus.

It raises a range of issues that you may like to ponder for yourself or discuss with others.

The following is not exhaustive and you may have more of your own, but here are a few questions that should get some good discussions started.

I would also advise you try to find Bible references to back up as many of your answers as possible, to ensure that all that is discussed is in line with the Word of God. To help with this, there are some additional Bible references to be found at www.robseabrook.com.

Chapter 1 – 'The Awakening'

- The perfect nature of heaven is fun to imagine. What do you imagine heaven may be like?
- What aspects of creation on earth do you find to be the most mesmerising? How may these be magnified in their beauty in a heavenly setting?
- What pointers to your imaginings can you find referenced in the Bible?
- In John 4:10 Jesus talks of himself giving us 'living water'. What do you think this means?
- Despite the clear promise from Jesus in Luke 23:43, *'I tell you the truth, today you will be with me in paradise'*, our central character wakes up in heaven but still doubts. How do you think you would react in this situation?
- What promises of Jesus do you doubt?

Chapter 2 – 'A New Beginning'

- In this chapter Jesus mentions he has many names. What names of God do you know? What do they mean and which of them can you personally relate to?
- Jesus mentions in the story that his Holy Spirit can take many forms. To ease the narrative and our understanding, in chapter two the Spirit takes the form of a young girl. What other forms do you think the Spirit can take? (Some are mentioned in the Bible.)
- Dismas clearly thinks that he does not deserve to be in heaven. Do you think he deserved to be there? Why?
- It may be unlikely that we will need to be baptised in heaven. But in this chapter it is a useful picture of our cleansing and renewal. It echoes Jesus' command in Mark 16:16 to believe and be baptised. What are your views of being baptised?
- In this book, Jesus comments that 'being a parent is such an important job'. In what ways do you agree with this?

Chapter 3 – 'Crowned with Splendour'

- Our main character feels a pang of guilt for remembering bad experiences when in heaven, as though they should have gone. How much of your life do you think you will remember in heaven? Will we forget the bad times or feel the pain of the bad experiences, when in heaven?
- How much do you think our childhood experiences affect us in our adult life, forming a key part of our personality? Can we ever fully recover from bad experiences?
- Names are important, a part of our self-identity and our identity in Christ. Jesus presents Habib with a white stone with his new name written on it, to help cement his new name in his heart. What do you think it means to have a new identity in Christ?

- A crown is one of the rewards of heaven mentioned in the Bible, with different crowns awarded to believers. Do you think there will be literal crowns in heaven? What other rewards of heaven do you think may be in store for us?

Chapter 4 – 'Alone in the Shadows'

- Habib comes across Jesus praying. Why would Jesus need to be praying? What do you think he could be praying about? What does this show us about the heart of Jesus?

- Habib mentions that the light in heaven is so different to what he has been used to. What do you think the source of light in heaven may be?

- 2 Corinthians 5:10 says, *'For we must all appear before the judgment seat of Christ, so that each of us may receive what is due to us for the things done while in the body, whether good or bad.'* See also Romans 14:10-12. In the story, the lapis lazuli plinth represents the judgment seat of God, a place where we recount our lives to Jesus. What do you think it will be like to have to recount all things you have said and done to Jesus, for his judgment?

- Then thinking about the loving and compassionate nature and intentions of God, how might you now reimagine it?

- Do you think that good deeds are necessary for your salvation? What Bible verses can you find to support your view?

Chapters 5 and 6 – 'A Sweet Fragrance' and 'Hope Destroyed'

- Riha gives Dismas 'the sky' for his birthday present. What aspects of creation speak to you most clearly about God's power and majesty, and feel to you like a gift from God?

- The poet Tennyson wrote the famous line: *'Tis better to have loved and lost, than never to have loved at all.* Do you think Dismas would agree?

- Towards the end of chapter six, the anger at his circumstances and loss begin to overwhelm Dismas. How do we start to deal with anger and bitterness in our lives?
- Riha was a companion for Dismas for a very short time, but she still made a big impact on him. How does fellowship with each other play a key role in our lives?
- At the end of chapter six, Dismas is helpless in being able to support Riha in her fight for life. How does helplessness affect our relationship with God?

Chapters 7 and 8 – 'Into the Depths' and 'Captured'

- Chapter seven begins with Habib soaking in the light (Ephesians 1:18) and receiving a revelation of hope from Jesus. Can you find hope in knowing that heaven may be a season of reunions and reconnections?
- Many would think that Dismas, as a street child and petty criminal, is completely insignificant. Knowing that he ends up in heaven, does that make you think differently about others that the 'world' may see as insignificant, or even yourself?
- Dismas' response to his situation is to lash out at the world and hate all around him for the trauma it has caused. If he had known Jesus' love for him during this hard time, how do you think his response may have been different?
- Dismas existed in a fallen world, as do we. How can we not get overwhelmed with the evil and suffering around us?

Chapter 9 – 'Reconnection'

- In Romans 10:9 it says: *If you declare with your mouth, 'Jesus is Lord,' and believe in your heart that God raised him from the dead, you will be saved.* And in Romans 10:13 it states: *Everyone who calls on the name of the Lord will be saved.* Do you believe that entering heaven is really this simple?

- Do you believe you are going to heaven? If so, why?
- Do you think you will be surprised to find out that some people like Dismas have 'made it' to heaven? In what ways does it challenge you, in realising that even those who have committed the worst wrongs, or behaved in the most detestable ways, can still be accepted into heaven?
- Forgiveness is a difficult concept to grasp, especially if we feel we have been the victim. Unforgiveness holds Habib back from being able to freely take communion. In what other ways does unforgiveness hold us back?
- Why do you think that extending forgiveness to people who have hurt you is important?
- Do you feel that some people's actions are impossible to forgive?
- Why do you think that taking the bread and wine is an important part of your relationship with God?

Chapters 10 and 11 – 'Condemned by the Law' and 'The Cross'

- The Jewish people were required to sacrifice a perfect lamb in order to receive forgiveness for their sins from God. What similarities can you see between this sacrifice and the death of Jesus on the cross?
- The horrific nature of crucifixion is often sanitised, but the reality is that it was brutal and vicious. Is it helpful to have a clearer knowledge of what Jesus went through in his punishments?
- What did Jesus actually achieve for us through his suffering and death?
- In the Old Testament there are many prophecies pointing to the

coming Messiah, his life and death. Can you think of any that are highlighted in the details of Jesus' death?

- Remembering the promise he received from Jesus when on the cross, at the point of his death, what do you think was Dismas' expectation of what would come next?

Chapter 12 – 'Restored'

- In this chapter, Jesus promises Habib that Father God does not abandon his children. But did Father God abandon his one and only Son, Jesus?
- Why do you think God asked Jesus to endure the cross?
- In this chapter, Jesus refers to children in heaven 'who come here early'. Do you think this happens?
- The Holy Spirit anoints Habib with oil, resulting in an outpouring of joy. Read Isaiah 61. What other promises of God can be released in us?
- Do you believe that Jesus knows your pain, has taken it upon himself and has dealt with it?

Chapter 13 – 'Homecoming'

- The angel's name, Shamar, means 'guardian'. What do you think about there being angels who battle for us and work to protect us? Can you find any biblical references to back this up?
- Habib does not see the face of God, but recognises him as being at the centre of heaven. Do you think we will be able to see the face of God in heaven?
- The whole of heaven is celebrating the return of Jesus and it erupts in worship. How would you describe worship?
- In heaven we will have complete freedom in our worship. Do you feel you have a similar freedom now? What might you begin to do in order to worship in a freer way?

- Habib's response to the heavenly celebration is for worship to rise from deep within him. Can you think of a time when your only response to God's majesty has been to worship?
- Habib is reunited with his mother and finally has a place in which he can abide for eternity. Jesus promises the same to us in John 14:2: *My Father's house has many rooms; if that were not so, would I have told you that I am going there to prepare a place for you?* How does this eternal promise reassure you?

Acknowledgements

I had always assumed that writing a book was a solitary task, but in writing my first book I now know that it takes a team to produce a project like this.

Thanks to the 'Alpha team', Hannah and Dan, for trawling through first, second and third drafts. You offered so much constructive feedback and helpful ideas that added to the story, as well as spotting the many typos, half-finished sentences and grammatical errors. To Amy, Dan B and Jan for reading through slightly more polished versions, which really helped to iron out the inconsistencies, heresies and fine tune it into a more presentable shape. Thanks to Heather B for her superb proof-reading skills, who made sure every 'i' was dotted and 't' was crossed. And thanks to the team at Malcolm Down Publishing for their diligence, great attention to detail and support in getting the finished article professionally published.

To Ella for the inspired artwork adorning the covers and the sketches introducing every chapter. Simply beautiful.

Thanks to Bruce and Heather T for their moral support and feedback on an early manuscript, and especially to Heather for giving me a conker one Sunday morning – the seed that sits on my desk and reminds me what power there is in a kernel of creativity.

Most of all, I could not have started or completed this project without the loving support from Gemma, who read through maybe eight or ten drafts, offered so much encouragement, tempered my excited ramblings and encouraged me to see it through when I felt I was just chasing a rainbow.

Finally, thanks to you for reading it. I hope it brings you some pleasure, insight and inspiration.